High Alert

by

Alex Lukeman

Copyright © 2017 by Alex Lukeman

http://www.alexlukeman.com

The Project Series:

White Jade
The Lance
The Seventh Pillar
Black Harvest
The Tesla Secret
The Nostradamus File
The Ajax Protocol
The Eye of Shiva
Black Rose
The Solomon Scroll
The Russian Deception
The Atlantis Stone
The Cup
High Alert

Be the first to know when I have a new book coming out by subscribing to my newsletter. No spam or busy emails, only a brief announcement now and then. Just click on the link below. You can unsubscribe at any time...

http://bit.ly/2kTBn85

The PROJECT is a counter-terrorism unit answering only to the President of the United States.

The Team

Elizabeth Harker: Director of the Project. Formerly part of the task force investigating 9/11 until sidelined for challenging the findings. Picked by the president to head up the Project for her independent thinking and sharp intelligence.

Nick Carter: Former major, USMC. The team leader in the field, with years of combat experience. Suffers from occasional PTSD and nightmares. He's got it more or less under control.

Selena Connor: Highly intelligent, a renowned linguist in ancient languages and expert in martial arts. Independently wealthy, the result of an inheritance. Introduced into Nick's violent world by accident, she is now a full fledged member of the Project team.

Lamont Cameron: Former Navy Seal, of Ethiopian descent. Expert in all things water related. His humorous attitude sometimes drives Elizabeth Harker to distraction. A tough cookie.

Ronnie Peete: Nick's oldest friend and a fellow RECON Marine. Expert with explosives, weapons and all things mechanical. A full blooded Navajo, Ronnie brings solidity and the wisdom of his culture to the team.

Stephanie Willits: Elizabeth Harker's deputy; computer guru. Stephanie maintains the Project's Cray computers. She can hack into any system as needed. Among other duties, she is responsible for the satellite communication network that keeps Harker up to speed and the team connected in the field.

PROLOGUE
Wonsan, North Korea
Present Time

The *USS California* lay submerged outside the harbor at Wonsan, home to North Korea's East Fleet. Captain Richard Paulson looked through the observation scope and didn't like what he saw. The harbor was crowded with patrol boats and small craft. That was normal. What wasn't normal were the hundreds of North Korean landing craft bobbing in the endless swell coming in from the Sea of Japan.

The DPRK's Great Leader was threatening again to invade the South. That was nothing new, but this time it looked as though there might be something to it. If Yun intended to carry through with his threats, it would begin with a launch from Wonsan.

The Pentagon wanted to know what the Koreans were up to, but the heavily guarded harbor was camouflaged to hide activity from the American satellites watching overhead. Paulson's mission orders were to get up close and observe. If the North sent those boats south, the mission would change to active deterrence.

USS California was an Ohio class ballistic missile submarine, modified for cruise missiles. She carried enough nuclear tipped Tomahawks to turn North Korea's armies into radioactive ash.

Paulson thought it was a mistake to place his multibillion-dollar submarine this close to North Korea's paranoid and sophisticated defenses, but orders were orders. Advanced stealth technology hid the sub from the North Korean sonic sweeps looking for someone like him hiding under the water. Even so, there was always a chance of being discovered.

Lots of activity. There are more of those craft than yesterday. They're getting ready to do something.

He rotated the scope, scanning the harbor and coastline. A thin, white wake trailed after the slender column.

Some things didn't work well in North Korea, but radar wasn't one of them. Lieutenant Kim Chul was the current duty officer responsible for surveillance of the exclusion zone outside the harbor. The enlisted man watching the radar display called out to him.

"What is it?"

"Sir, I think there's a sub outside the harbor."

"One of ours?"

"No sir, I don't think so. She made no recognition signals."

Kim came over to the screen. "Show me."

"Here, sir." He pointed. "That looks like a periscope to me."

The radar man indicated the distinctive signature on the screen. Suddenly it was gone.

"What about the sonar net? Any sign?"

"No, sir."

Kim's authority did not extend to ordering countermeasures. That required a higher rank. He picked up the direct phone to headquarters and asked for the base commander.

Admiral Park Hwan had served the Great Leader's father before him. Not inclined to question the orders of his superiors, Park could be relied upon to do what was needed. In a country saturated in suspicion and paranoia, he was one of a very few high-ranking officers still trusted. It was why he'd been given his important job. He had made it a point to encourage the lower ranks to speak with him first in the event of a serious breach of security. It was why Kim was able to call him directly. To Kim's knowledge, no one had ever done so, but he wasted no time making the call.

"Yes."

"Sir, this is the Harbor Surveillance Duty Officer, Lieutenant Kim. Radar has spotted what appears to be a hostile submarine lying offshore. A periscope was detected."

"You are certain?"

Kim took a deep breath. If he was wrong he would soon be headed for one of the rehabilitation camps.

"I am not absolutely certain, sir. But I believe it was a submarine. It can't be one of ours. None of ours are in the area. From the signature, I think it's American."

"An American submarine is suspected to be in the vicinity. Very well. Return to your post. We'll take care of it. But you'd better be right."

"Sir."

Kim set the phone down. His hand was sweating. *You'd better be right.*

"Watch for any further anomalies," he said to the radar operator.

"Sir."

They'll send patrol boats, Kim thought, *with depth charges.*

Admiral Park unlocked a drawer in his desk and took out a manila envelope stamped with the red code for state secrets. Up until now, there had been no need to follow the orders contained within it.

The orders came from the Supreme Leader himself. It would do no good to point out the complications that would come if they were carried out. No one contradicted the Supreme Leader or suggested that his judgment was anything but perfect. Not unless they wanted to end up in front of a firing squad.

Or worse.

Park got up from his desk and grunted in pain, feeling the ache of his arthritic knees. He picked up the envelope and crossed the hall to the operations center. All communications, defense systems and combat related operations were coordinated in this room, kept fully staffed around the clock. The communications area took up one entire side of the large space. Along with the radar, radio and satellite communications were as good as what the Chinese had, which was very good indeed. That wasn't a mystery. Almost all the gear had been manufactured in China and the operators trained by their military counterparts from Beijing.

Admiral Park went to the radio officer in charge, a man named Bak. His shoulder boards bore the single star and two red stripes of a Lieutenant Commander. Bak sprang to attention at the admiral's approach. The admiral was proud of his men and knew they respected him. Respect was everything. They would follow his orders without question.

"Sir."

Park withdrew a single sheet of paper from the manila envelope. It contained a radio frequency and a string of computer code.

"There is a possible enemy submarine lying submerged offshore. I want you to transmit this to them."

"Sir, excuse me, but our transmissions will not reach them unless they have raised an aerial."

"Don't worry about that. Send the coding on that frequency. It will reach them, if they are there."

Bak looked at the frequency. "Ah. At once, sir."

He took the paper to an enlisted man sitting at a nearby console.

"Send this immediately."

"Sir."

The radio operator raised his eyebrows when he saw the frequency. He entered it and began transmitting. After a minute he was done.

"Will there be a reply, sir?" the operator asked.

Admiral Park had come up to stand near Bak.

"I don't think so," he said.

In the waters of Wonsan Bay, an underwater drone awoke. Its American codename was *Black Dolphin.* The North Koreans had renamed it *Righteous Anger.* Lieutenant Commander Bak's transmission told the drone to seek for a possible submerged submarine.

The drone went into hunting mode and detected the enormous shape of *California* hiding outside the harbor. It slid quietly through the water and attached itself to the hull with a dull thud that sounded through the ship.

On board the submarine, someone said, "What was that?"

The computer inside the drone released a device to penetrate the stealth material covering the outside of the sub, then began transmitting high-speed bursts of code using the metallic hull of the submarine as an antenna.

The Chief of Watch was monitoring the functions of the ship at his station. Now he turned to the captain, alarmed.

"Sir, someone is accessing our computers."

"What? That's not possible."

Across the compartment, the Chief Petty Officer supervising the combat control consoles called out.

"Sir, I'm starting to lose functions. Were being hacked."

"Block it. Now!"

"Aye, Sir."

The CPO's hands flew over his keyboard as he tried to compensate for the interference.

"Sir, the computer is dumping memory."

There was a hint of panic in his voice. Alarms began sounding throughout the boat. Computer displays in the control room began to go dark, one by one. The emergency lighting flickered on.

"Damn it, man, stop them."

"Sir..."

With sudden, ominous movement, the sub tilted sharply down. Captain Paulson was thrown across the compartment and hard into a bulkhead. He lay where he'd fallen, unconscious. Shouts and cries came from other parts of the boat.

The submarine went into a vertical dive.

Then all the lights went out.

CHAPTER 1

Nick Carter parked outside Project Headquarters under a dark sky spitting flurries of snow. The sun was nowhere to be seen. It was only the first week of December, but the weather was well into another miserable East Coast winter. He stepped out of the warmth of the car and the cold slapped him, making him feel every one of his forty-two years. By the time he reached the entrance of the building and waited for the identity scan, his old wounds were aching.

He took off his coat and hung it on a Victorian style hall rack and mirror in the entry foyer. The face staring back at him from the mirror had dark circles under the eyes. He hadn't had much sleep in the last weeks. Not since he'd returned from Syria. Nick peered at his reflection and rubbed the scarred end of his left ear, where the lobe had been sacrificed to a Chinese bullet.

Touches of gray had begun showing up in his hair. He'd decided to let it grow a little and was still getting used to the new look. He wasn't getting used to the gray.

His boss was in Walter Reed, in a coma after a car accident that had almost killed her. No one was sure when Elizabeth Harker would wake up. Until she returned Nick was in charge of the project with Stephanie Willits, Harker's deputy. He'd come in early to try and get a handle on the day. He went into Harker's office and sat down at her desk.

A huge orange tomcat strolled over and rubbed against Nick's leg, shedding hair over the gray carpet. The cat purred, a loud rumble that reminded Nick of a miniature Mack truck.

"Hey, Burps. Hungry?"

The cat looked up and drooled and purred. Nick stood and went to a cabinet by the coffee machine and took out a can of cat food. He opened it up, dumped the food in a dish and set it on the floor with a bowl of water. He turned on the coffee and went back to the desk while Burps began gulping down breakfast. While he waited for the coffee to brew, Nick leaned back in Elizabeth's chair and closed his eyes, fighting off fatigue.

Ever since he'd returned from Syria, things had been in turmoil. The mission had been difficult enough. The aftermath had been confusing. Something had changed, but he wasn't sure what it was. The closest he could come was that he felt a little less pessimistic about what was happening in the world, a little more hopeful that somehow things would work out.

Running the Project meant endless mental tasks that took time and concentration. A mistake in judgment could cost lives, even contribute to starting a war. Nick thought it was a lot clearer in the field, when people were shooting at you. Then you knew what you had to do. This was different. It would've been overwhelming except for help from Clarence Hood, Director of the CIA.

The Project's relationship with Langley had been contentious for years, until the former director had been exposed as a traitor and Hood had taken over. In recent weeks, Hood and Elizabeth Harker had gotten involved in a relationship that went beyond their professional interaction.

The CIA and the Project were bound together in more ways than one. Stephanie was married to

Lucas Monroe, the Director of National Clandestine Services at Langley.

Damn near incestuous, Nick thought.

The smell of coffee filled the office. Nick pulled himself out of the chair, went to the counter and poured a cup. He walked over to the patio doors with the cup in his hand and looked out over the grounds. The flowerbeds had retreated into winter mode, brown and sere, poking through a covering of snow from the last storm.

The flurries had changed to snow. Nick sipped his coffee and looked up at the row of clocks on the wall across from the desk. The rest of the Project team would arrive sometime during the next hour.

The secured phone on the desk signaled a call. Nick looked at the blinking light.

Langley. Here we go, he thought. He picked up.

"This is Carter."

"Good morning, Nick, although it could be better." It was Clarence Hood. "We have a problem."

"What's happened?"

"We've lost one of our cruise missile subs off North Korea. The *California* went down nineteen hours ago with all her crew."

"Everyone?"

"Yes."

"What happened?"

"That's what I'm calling about. It wasn't an accident. We think North Korea is responsible."

"The North Koreans sank her? Are they out of their minds?"

"Intelligence suggests Yun is getting ready to invade the South. The *California* was keeping an eye on the harbor at Wonsan."

"Where they're building up an invasion fleet," Nick said. It wasn't a question.

"Exactly. The DPRK is good at hiding things from our satellites. The Pentagon wanted direct visual sighting to confirm our intelligence and we don't have any assets on the ground to verify. *California's* mission was to observe and stay out of the way."

"Are we certain it was Pyongyang and not an accident?" Nick asked.

"It definitely wasn't an accident," Hood said. "She was sunk using our own technology. No one else is supposed to have it. The emergency buoy recorded what happened to her and transmitted the information when it reached the surface. Transmissions have stopped. The North Koreans plucked it out of the water."

"What kind of technology?"

"Now that you're acting in Elizabeth's place, I can tell you. DARPA developed an underwater drone called *Black Dolphin* that attaches itself to the hull of an enemy ship. It hacks into the target's computers and shuts them down. On the surface, a ship would lose all computer-controlled functions. It would drift, helpless. With a submarine, she'd turn into a big rock. That's what happened to *California.*"

"How do the North Koreans come to have our top-secret tech?"

"That's the question, isn't it?"

"Treason," Nick said. "Someone gave it to them."

"It's the only possibility. Not only that, no one could break through the firewalls on one of our nuclear subs without the right codes. It has to be someone high up in the command structure with access to that information."

"At least it narrows the field."

"We'll find him, whoever it is," Hood said.

"What happens next?"

"President Rice isn't going to let the North Koreans get away with this. It may be up to his successor to finish what he starts, but Rice is mounting a rescue mission in case some of our people are still alive. The sub went down in North Korean waters. Yun is unstable, no one knows how he'll react. This could trigger a war."

President Rice was in the last days of his second term. It remained to be seen what would happen when the newly elected president took office. No one knew what approach he would take toward the covert world where the Project operated, or the black budget that funded it.

"China won't like this," Nick said.

"You just put your finger on one of the problems. The Chinese have been unwilling to shut down Yun's lunacy with his missiles and his nuclear program. Now it's coming back to bite them in the ass. They're worried we're going to provoke him into using his nukes."

"So it's our fault if he does?"

"Everything is our fault, these days. There's a meeting at the White House with the Chinese ambassador later today to discuss the situation. President Zhang will be on the phone. Rice wants Selena in the room with him, to listen in."

Selena Connor was part of the field team. Against all the odds, she and Nick had gotten married the year before. Selena spoke Chinese fluently and understood the important nuances lost or omitted in translation. Her uncle had been a close friend of the president, and she'd known Rice since she was a child. He'd asked her once before to help him understand the minds of the men who ran China.

"She'll be here soon," Nick said. "What time is the meeting?"

"Four o'clock. Rice wants her at the White House a half hour before, and he wants you and your team outside. There will be protests when the story leaks."

"The Secret Service can handle it. We're not cops. Why would he need us? Did it occur to him that I'm a little busy right now?"

"Ours but to do or die, Nick. What the president wants, he gets."

After he hung up, Nick leaned back and thought about the *California*. Someone had given the North Koreans the technology. Whoever he was, Nick hoped the bastard was found out before he did any more damage.

He heard the door open and someone stomping their feet in the entryway. A moment later Lamont Cameron came in. He threw his coat over the arm of the couch across from Harker's desk and sat down.

"Man, I hate this cold weather. How about coming up with a mission someplace warm?"

"Scuttlebutt says we might be heading to the Arctic," Nick said.

"Funny, Nick. You got a real future as a comedian."

Lamont was one of four who composed the Project team in the field, along with Nick, Selena, and Ronnie Peete. He was a little shorter than Nick's six feet, lean and muscled. He'd been a Navy SEAL for most of his military career and had the scars to prove it.

Shrapnel in Iraq had left a long, pink line across his brown face. It started over his right eyebrow and worked its way across the bridge of his nose, then down his left cheek. It gave him a piratical look that belied his easy-going humor.

Selena and Ronnie came in the door and shook snow off their boots. A puddle of water was starting to collect in the entry.

"I don't think the snow's going to last," Ronnie said as he sat down. "It doesn't smell like it. Just enough to make everything a mess."

"With that nose of yours, I'll take that as gospel," Lamont said.

"It is a Roman nose," Ronnie said, "a sign of intelligence and intuition." He sniffed. "The snow will stop."

It was true Ronnie had a big nose. It went with his Navajo heritage. He had the stocky build, light brown skin, broad shoulders and narrow hips of the People. He dropped onto the couch next to Lamont. Selena sat next to him.

The dress code at Project HQ was casual. Selena wore black slacks and boots. She had on a dark blue sweater that brought out the violet color of her eyes, She wore no jewelry except her wedding ring. The cut of her red-blonde hair framed high cheekbones hinting at a Slavic ancestor in the distant past. She had the kind of unselfconscious beauty that always got a second look. A natural beauty mark above her lip added the final touch.

Nick wasn't used to looking at the team from this side of Elizabeth's desk. He wasn't comfortable with the feeling of separation it created, but it went with the territory.

A friendly looking, dark-haired woman came into the room and took a seat near the desk.

Stephanie Willits knew how the Washington political game worked. She was Elizabeth's deputy and knew where all the bodies were buried. Technically, she should have been the one sitting in Harker's chair, but she and Nick had played this game before. There wasn't any competition between them. They shared a mutual determination to get the job done. She took her usual seat to the right of the desk.

She'd arranged for someone to stay with her newborn son during the day while she was working. Normally, Steph was full of energy. Today she seemed tired, her cheerful face showing the stress of a newborn baby and holding down one of the toughest jobs in Washington.

"Sorry I'm late. Matthew kept me up half the night."

"It's nothing to worry about, Steph."

Nick decided to begin the meeting and get right to the point.

"I got a call from DCI Hood this morning to start off our day. There's a problem."

"There's always a problem," Ronnie said.

"Yesterday one of our ballistic subs went down with all hands," Nick said. "The *California* carried a hundred and sixty-five officers and enlisted men and a full complement of nuclear cruise missiles."

Lamont sighed. "Shit. I have a buddy on the *California.*"

"How? Where was she?" Selena asked. She brushed a wisp of hair away from her face. It was a gesture Nick had come to love.

"The how is what we're going to talk about. The where is off the East Coast of North Korea, in twenty-seven hundred feet of water."

"Did the Koreans sink her?"

"Almost certainly. They're the logical suspects at this point."

"Do we know what happened?" Lamont asked.

"Yes and no. We know some of it. Her emergency beacon deployed when she went down. Aside from giving the location, the beacon records all the relevant data and functions of the vessel up to the moment it's released."

"Like an airplane black box?" Selena asked.

"Right, only more sophisticated. When there's an accident and the beacon reaches the surface, it broadcasts everything to a satellite. The *California's* beacon sent everything it had recorded before the North Koreans retrieved it."

"Have we mounted a rescue operation?"

"Yes. That's part of the problem. She was patrolling outside Wonsan harbor. Pyongyang is claiming it's a provocation for war and using it as a propaganda tool."

"Crush depth on those big nuclear subs is just under twenty-two hundred feet," Lamont said, "but she might survive deeper than that. The crew could still be alive."

"It's possible. We can hope so, but that's not our job. It's a touchy situation because North Korea's leader is unpredictable. Nobody knows what he's going to do."

"Why did you say yes and no about how she was sunk?" Selena asked.

"The sub went down because a virus was transmitted into her computers. We know that because of the record on the beacon. That's the 'yes' part."

"I thought you couldn't transmit something like that underwater," Lamont said.

"Usually you can't. Salt water blocks transmission of everything except very low-frequency or extremely low frequency transmissions. The virus wasn't sent in that manner. Before the sub's computers failed, the emergency buoy recorded a distinct signature. It was done using a top-secret device developed by our own people."

"What kind of device?" Ronnie asked.

He settled his broad shoulders against the couch and rubbed his nose.

"An underwater drone codenamed *Black Dolphin.* It's programmed to attach itself to an enemy vessel and transmit the virus, using the hull as an antenna. Hood told me about it when we talked on the phone this morning. Technically none of you are cleared to know about it. You can't mention it to anyone."

"Wait a minute," Lamont said. "The computers on our nuclear subs have so many firewalls no one could get through them without the proper codes."

Nick just looked at him.

"Oh, boy," Lamont said. "Someone gave the Koreans the codes?"

Nick nodded. "Yes. What we don't know is who it was. That's the 'no' part, Selena. Whoever it was, there's a traitor somewhere in our command structure."

"Those are strong words, Nick," Ronnie said.

"There isn't any other explanation. That technology is as secret as it gets. Only a high-ranking officer would know the codes or be able to access plans for the drone."

"We're certain about what happened?" Stephanie asked.

"The beacon recorded a specific signature that identifies *Black Dolphin*. The computers on the sub were compromised and taken off-line. They wouldn't have had time to do much of anything before the ship went into negative buoyancy and headed down."

"Where do we come in?"

"I'm not sure yet, but you can bet Rice will come up with something. He isn't going to walk away from those men. He's gone to DEFCON 2."

"That was fast," Ronnie said.

"The whole situation is dangerous as hell," Nick said. "North Korea's so-called Great Leader seems to be getting ready to invade the South. That's why *California* was lying off Wonsan, to observe their preparations."

"Here we go again," Lamont said. "That guy is a nut job. He never quits."

"If Pyongyang invades the South, it brings China into the mix," Selena said. "Not to mention Russia. Orlov won't sit on the sidelines."

Nick nodded. "Beijing knows we won't permit the North to conquer South Korea. We'd intervene, as we did in the 50s. It's not in Beijing's interest to see a war start between North and South Korea, but you can be damn sure they don't want us taking over the peninsula."

"We could be looking at another Korean War," Selena said.

"You mean the police action no one wants to call a war?" Ronnie said.

"Rice spoke with China's President Zhang an hour ago and told him we think North Korea sank the sub. He told him we're going to send a rescue mission whether Pyongyang agrees or not, and that we will defend against any effort to keep us from doing so. Advance elements of the Seventh Fleet are already on their way from Yokosuka. If the North Koreans start shooting, we'll shoot back."

"I bet that made Zhang's day," Ronnie said.

"Zhang may decide China has to assist her ally. Or he could pressure Yun not to interfere with the rescue mission. He could decide they've had enough with Yun's erratic behavior and take over the North entirely. That's another scenario we won't tolerate. Whatever happens, if we start trading shots with the North Koreans it could lead to a confrontation with China."

"The Korean War was a long time ago," Ronnie said. "Everything is different now."

"Missiles and nukes are what's different," Nick said. "If a war starts between North and South, it's going to escalate. Yun can't win, but he's crazy and arrogant enough to think he can. He believes his enormous army could take Seoul in a few days. He'd be right, except for the fact that we guarantee South Korea's safety. He has nukes, as he's always telling everyone. If he thinks he's going to lose, he'll use them."

Selena said, "Where do we fit in?"

"Remember how we helped the Chinese avoid a coup?"

"How could I forget?"

That mission had brought Nick and Selena together. The high mountains of Tibet and an ancient fortress guarding an emperor's tomb had been the scene of Selena's initiation into combat.

"Rice and Zhang have scheduled a teleconference this afternoon at the White House. The Chinese are as worried about war in Korea as we are. The Chinese ambassador will be there as Zhang's personal representative. Rice wants you to listen when he talks to Zhang. He trusts you. It's not just because you understand Chinese. It's because of your intuition, your ability to sense what's being said behind the words."

"I'm flattered, but he's overestimating my ability."

"I don't think he is. Remember the last time."

"What about the rest of us?" Lamont asked.

"There will be protests when word leaks out about the sub. Anything to do with North Korea, the Chinese, or nuclear submarines brings people out on the street. The rest of us will be on the scene and liaise with the Secret Service while Rice is talking to Zhang."

Lamont said, "Those boys are pretty territorial. They'll have us guarding the White House outhouse."

"There's an outhouse?" Ronnie said.

"If there isn't, they'll probably build one for us."

"We'll work with them, not for them," Nick said. "I don't know why Rice wants us there, but we don't have a choice about it. We'll be outside. If there's going to be trouble, that's where it will happen.. People always want someone to blame for the mess we're in and there are powerful interests happy to oblige them."

"It's not as though Zhang will be here in person," Selena said.

"His ambassador will. Now that Rice's administration is on its way out the door, the White House is springing more leaks than the Titanic. Someone will organize a demonstration. It could be about Tibet or nuclear power or about American neo-colonialism in Korea. It doesn't matter."

"What a great country," Lamont said.

"You know, Nick, you don't have to go with us," Ronnie said. "This is just a dog and pony show, nothing's going to happen."

"I need a break from this desk," Nick said. "Besides, Rice asked for me to be there with everyone else."

"Yeah, but you're supposed to be running things, not doing grunt work like this."

"Hey, I have to keep an eye on you, don't I?"

CHAPTER 2

The sinking of *USS California* leaked before noon. The White House Press Secretary announced that a rescue mission had been dispatched from Japan. He went on to say that, Rice would talk later in the day with the President of China to discuss "regional stability," and that the Chinese ambassador had been invited to the White House to participate in the call.

By two o'clock there were more than a thousand people outside the barriers on Pennsylvania Avenue in front of the White House. They carried homemade signs protesting nuclear weapons, climate change, and the Chinese occupation of Tibet. An hour later new signs appeared, printed to look as though they were homemade. Those called for the withdrawal of U.S. troops from South Korea.

The weather had warmed and turned the snow to slush underfoot. Nick and the others waited where East Street intersected 17th on the west side of the White House grounds. The Secret Service wasn't happy about their presence but there wasn't much they could do about it. Rice wanted Nick and the others on hand and that was the end of it.

Movable barriers manned by city police blocked all the cross streets. Ambassador Li would come up 17th from Constitution Avenue, avoiding the growing mob on Pennsylvania Avenue. From there he would enter the White House grounds on E, turn onto West Executive Avenue and go through the Southwest appointment gate, continuing until he reached the entrance to the West Wing.

Selena was already inside. Agents had taken her straight to the situation room, where President Rice would take Zhang's call.

Nick and Ronnie stood watching the scene. Lamont walked over, his hands crammed deep in the pockets of his coat. He wore a woolen watch cap and had a thick scarf wrapped around his neck.

"I feel like a fifth wheel," he said. "They don't want us here."

He gestured at two Secret Service agents nearby. They looked as though they'd sprung from the same pod, both hatless and wearing dark overcoats, polished shoes spattered by slush, sunglasses and earpieces trailing white, coiled cords from their ears. They did their best to ignore Nick and the others. The feeling was mutual.

"You can't blame them," Nick said. "They've got their job to do. As far as they're concerned, we're just one more thing to keep an eye on."

Ronnie said. "At least most of the crowd is out front."

Lamont pointed at a growing crowd of about a hundred people standing on the other side of the police barrier where E Street intersected 17th before it entered the White House grounds.

"Yeah, but some of them figured out that the action might be down here."

"They look cold," Ronnie said. "Check out the Asian guy standing in front. He's bundled up like he thinks he's in Alaska."

One of the Secret Service agents touched his earpiece and said something. He and his partner looked south toward Constitution Avenue.

"Heads up," Nick said. "The Chinese ambassador is getting close."

A black limousine turned onto 17th Street. Flags of the Chinese People's Republic flew from the front fenders. Across the way, there was a ripple in the crowd waiting on the other side of the barrier. They began shouting and waving signs.

"Free Tibet! Free Tibet! Free Tibet!"

The limousine slowed to turn onto the White House grounds. The bundled man Ronnie had pointed out suddenly leapt over the portable barrier. He ran toward the car, threw himself on the hood, and vanished in a violent explosion of sound and flame.

The blast knocked Nick off his feet. The wreckage of the limo coasted a few feet and stopped. A great balloon of black smoke billowed up toward the gray sky overhead.

Nick braced his hand on the wet ground and got up on one knee. Lamont stumbled over and helped him up. He was saying something. Nick watched his lips move but couldn't hear anything.

Nick pointed at his ear. "I can't hear you." His voice was a muffled echo inside his head.

The smoking remains of the ambassador's limousine looked as though someone had reached down with a giant hand and ripped it open. The top was peeled back like the lid of a tin can. Nothing remained of the interior but twisted metal coated with blood and bits of flesh. The doors were blown open. An unattached foot wearing a shiny shoe lay nearby on the pavement. Blood trickled from the open doors.

There were flecks of blood on Nick's coat. Across the way, some of the demonstrators stood dazed while others moved aimlessly in shock. Someone was on her knees, crying. There were bodies lying on the ground. One of the Secret

Service agents was down, his partner yelling into his microphone.

Somewhere, a siren sounded.

CHAPTER 3

In a secure Moscow enclave reserved for high-ranking government officials, General Alexei Ivanovitch Vysotsky was having an uneasy dream, watching a huddle of men whispering about him. They kept glancing in his direction, giving him unfriendly looks. One of them took an old-fashioned phone from his pocket with a rotary dial and spun the dial with his finger. The phone made a persistent buzzing noise.

"Stop that," Vysotsky said in the dream.

The man held the phone up and grinned at him, his mouth full of steel teeth.

The buzzing kept up. Alexei opened his eyes. The cell phone on the table next to his bed was vibrating in a circle. He reached for it.

"Yes."

He listened for a moment.

"Yes," he said again. "Right away."

He broke the connection and put the phone back on the table.

The director of SVR, Russia's Foreign Intelligence Service, sat up in bed and rubbed sleep out of his eyes. The call had summoned him to the Kremlin and informed him about the attack in Washington. It promised a bad day ahead.

Vysotsky used the bathroom. As he shaved, the face staring back from the mirror reflected the burden that came with power in Russia. The last year had left deep lines on his wide, peasant face, accenting the heavy eyebrows and dark eyes bequeathed to him by his forebears. His hair, once black as coal, was showing streaks of silver and beginning to recede.

He thought about the threats he was monitoring. The American Seventh Fleet was steaming toward North Korea. The separatists were creating trouble in Chechnya again. A new shipment of missiles had arrived in the Ukraine, courtesy of the West. And now the Chinese ambassador to Washington had been blown to bits as he entered the White House grounds.

Vysotsky had never met the ambassador, but he knew about him. It was his business to know. A personal friend of President Zhang, Ambassador Li had been adept at presenting a face of China to the world that was enlightened and friendly. He'd been skillful in diverting attention from the serpent coiled behind the public actions of Beijing.

Trouble, Vysotsky thought. *Zhang will take action. Who will he blame? What will he do?*

The President of the Russian Federation was certain to ask. Vysotsky needed to answer those questions for himself before he arrived at Vladimir Orlov's office in the Kremlin compound.

Vysotsky summoned his aide.

"Colonel Zhukov. Have the car ready. I am called to the Kremlin."

"At once, sir."

Zhukov clicked his heels together and left the room.

Alexei dressed quickly in a fresh uniform. Shoulder boards with three stars marked him as a Colonel General, promotion that had come with his elevation to Director of SVR. Alexei was now one of the most powerful men in the Federation, but he was under no illusions as to where the source of his power lay. In things that counted, not much had changed since the days of the Soviet Union. Orlov had lifted him up and could as easily cut him down. As long as Alexei found ways to advance the president's agenda for a resurgent Russia, he was reasonably safe.

When he'd finished dressing, Alexei called his headquarters in Yasenevo and started the process to discover who was responsible for the assassination. He'd find out, sooner or later. Once SVR began looking, few things could remain hidden.

A corporal stood by the door with a thermos of hot tea. There was vodka in the limousine if Vysotsky wanted it.

Alexei shrugged on a heavy greatcoat and donned his high peaked officer's hat. He held the thermos in one gloved hand and stepped out into the Arctic cold of Moscow. His limo idled in the courtyard of the residential compound, sending a steady stream of exhaust fog into the early morning air. He climbed into the back and pulled the heavy armor-plated door shut.

The heater was going full blast, but it was still cold in the car. He unscrewed the top of the thermos and poured tea. It was laced with brandy, the way he liked it. He sipped and felt welcome warmth slide down his throat. The car pulled smoothly away from the compound, heading for the Kremlin.

Vysotsky's lavish apartment was located in the district of Dorogomilovo, twenty minutes away from the Kremlin. By the time he arrived, he needed to have suggestions ready for the man who ran Russia.

He considered the implications of the attack. The more he thought about it, the more he was certain it could turn into something bigger than the death of an important diplomat. Everyone in Beijing was touchy, these days. By the time the car reached the walls of the Kremlin, he still wasn't sure what he was going to say. He'd take his cue from Orlov and hope for the best.

Vladimir Orlov's office was located in the green-domed Senate building in the northern end of the Kremlin compound. The snow had been cleared away in front of the building, exposing the icy stones of the courtyard. Two guards carrying AK 74s saluted as Vysotsky approached and held open the tall doors of the entrance for him. Inside, an aide took his hat and greatcoat.

"He's waiting for you, General," the aide said.

Vysotsky grunted and strode across the polished floor to the office of Russia's president.

Orlov sat at a desk inlaid with Ukrainian malachite, the same desk used by Khrushchev during the Cuban missile crisis. More than five decades had passed since Khrushchev had blinked and withdrawn the missiles. Orlov considered it one of Russia's deepest humiliations. It was why he'd ordered the desk brought out of storage and placed in his office when he'd come to power. He intended to redeem his predecessor's mistake while sitting behind it.

The president's office was a study in 18th century architecture, a remnant of the days of the Czars. A large crystal chandelier hung from a high, curved ceiling painted with beige triangles and squares outlined in white. Carved cornices painted white marched along the junction between wall and ceiling at studied intervals.

The floor was composed of inlaid hardwoods, much of it covered by a Persian rug woven in an elaborate floral pattern. The walls were lined with brown oak panels and tall, glass fronted bookcases.

Displayed on the wall behind Orlov's desk was the golden double-headed eagle and crest of the Russian Federation. Two flags flanked the wall to either side of the eagle. To Orlov's left, a large window looked out over the courtyard.

The President of the Russian Federation was of average height, with manicured hands that were almost dainty. His eyes were blue and cold as the Arctic sky. He wore a perfectly tailored blue suit and a blue and white striped tie. An enameled pin with the Russian flag adorned his lapel.

Orlov was well muscled under his politician's suit, something he worked at in his private gym. He'd taken his cue from Mao and liked to show the public that he was a powerful man. He made sure he was seen doing things that enhanced his image of strength and masculinity. He'd been photographed hunting in Siberia, swimming the Moscow River in winter, arm wrestling with the Army champion.

When the Soviet Union collapsed, Orlov had resigned from the KGB and gone into politics. The system he'd grown up with was no more, but his ties to the fraternity of the Sword and Shield and his belief in its philosophy had never changed. Neither had his attitude toward those he considered to be Russia's enemies.

There were many of those, China and America first among them. The murder of the Chinese ambassador was an opportunity to increase dissension between them. It remained to be seen how the situation could be exploited.

Orlov understood the cruel and passionate love his country demanded and shared the paranoia toward outsiders that was ingrained in the Russian soul. Like many Russians, he believed that only a strong leader backed by a powerful military could restore the prestige Russia had once held. As other dictators had done before him, he'd used the trappings of democracy to give himself legitimacy.

Though Western propaganda often depicted Orlov as a KGB thug of limited ability, nothing was farther from the truth. Playing the game of Russian politics at Orlov's level required much more than cunning and the will to be ruthless. It also required a particular kind of dark genius. His presidency depended on managing the oligarchs and the military, the two factions that determined who led the Federation. Without their backing, no one could remain in power in modern Russia.

He had satisfied the generals by modernizing much of the Russian military. He'd improved conditions, increased pay and increased the size of the armed forces. Better equipment, better tanks, and new weapons were pouring off the production lines. Russian forces once again wore their uniforms with pride. The annexation of Crimea had pleased the generals. The military was firmly on his side, anticipating expansion into Ukraine and Eastern Europe.

The oligarchs had been a different kind of challenge. Orlov persuaded those who questioned his authority that patriotic duty required turning over some of their ill gotten assets to the state. Unspoken was the certain knowledge that doing their duty assured their health and well-being. Those who'd opposed him during his first term had met with unfortunate accidents or investigations and imprisonment. Others had fled the country in self-imposed exile. The message had been received. Things were now running smoothly.

All in all, it had turned out well for Vladimir Orlov.

As Vysotsky entered, Orlov half stood and gestured at a chair in front of his desk.

"General."

"Mister President."

"Sit down, Alexei."

"Sir." Alexei sat.

Orlov could be devious or not. This time, he chose directness.

"I want to know who is responsible for assassinating the Chinese ambassador."

"I have given orders to find out," Vysotsky said.

"I would expect no less. It will have occurred to you that this is an opportunity for us."

Alexei nodded, but in fact had not yet considered what particular advantage the assassination might offer. He hedged with his reply.

"The Chinese will be very angry," he said. "I don't think they will blame the Americans, but relations with Washington will be strained at exactly the time when the White House needs the help of Beijing with that lunatic in Pyongyang."

"What is the status of the American rescue operation?"

"Elements of the Seventh Fleet are nearing North Korea's territorial waters. Rice is serious about attempting a rescue. My information is that he will not allow the North Koreans to interfere with the operation. Any effort to do so will be met with all force necessary. There is a real risk of war."

"What about Yun? Do you think he'll take that path?"

"Something is seriously wrong with that man," Vysotsky said. "He's unpredictable, but in my opinion he can't back down. There are elements in his military watching for signs of weakness. If he doesn't stand up to the Americans, he risks being deposed. Their sub went down near the Headquarters of the East Fleet. Yun has sent ships to the area. Their job is to prevent anyone from getting close."

"The Americans will turn his little boats into scrap metal if he starts shooting at them," Orlov said.

"Unless China intervenes on his behalf. Mister President, this is a very dangerous situation. Yun has enough missiles to do serious damage to the Americans. If he uses them they will retaliate. Beijing will be very nervous after the events in Washington. If China decides to get involved, things could escalate quickly. You mentioned that this could be an opportunity for us. I agree, but war in Korea is not to our advantage."

Orlov steepled his fingers together and leaned back in his chair.

"You believe Yun will not allow the Americans to launch their rescue."

"I think it's likely he will not. But as I said, he's unpredictable. He may decide a magnanimous gesture is a better decision than the humiliation of certain defeat, assuming he understands the concept of defeat in the first place. I'm not sure that he does."

"What do you suggest, General?"

"Sir, I think we must find a way to intervene. Early winter and floods are already creating big problems in the North. Yun needs heavy machinery, food, fuel. We could bribe him. Offer him what he needs. Point out to him the international approval he would gain by allowing the United States to try and rescue their submariners. Offer some sort of ongoing aid he can use to help him maintain power."

Orlov laughed. "I had no idea of your diplomatic potential, General. A bribe. It might work. I agree that war on the peninsula is not to our advantage at this time. Beijing will see it as interference, however."

"The Chinese don't want a war in Korea any more than we do," Vysotsky said. "Yun might not respond to an offer from us, but Beijing could make the approach. Perhaps we could provide the supplies needed and the Chinese could take the credit. If they can persuade Yun to cooperate, it increases his obligation to them. Yun could claim that the sinking was an unfortunate accident and that he allowed the rescue in the name of common humanity. Both Yun and the Chinese would save face and avoid confronting the Americans. It also gives us a chip with the Chinese for the future."

"I see that I was correct in promoting you to your position."

"Thank you, Mister President."

"What happened to that American submarine?"

"It's possible they had a system malfunction, an accident."

"You don't sound very convinced, General."

"We picked up the transmission from the submarine's emergency buoy. Something happened to the computers and took all of them off-line within seconds. The sub never had a chance. There has been recent intelligence indicating that the Americans have developed an underwater weapon that can cripple a ship's electronic systems."

"They wouldn't use it against their own vessel."

"Of course not, but perhaps they were testing it and something went wrong."

"What is the status of your current operation in the Ukraine?"

Orlov was referring to a plan to kill the Ukrainian chief of internal security and counterintelligence. Vysotsky noticed that Orlov had used the word "your" rather than "our." The fact that Orlov had ordered the assassination would make no difference if the attempt failed. Vysotsky would be the one who paid the price.

"Everything is on schedule."

"Good."

Orlov stood. Vysotsky rose with him.

"Find out who killed the Chinese ambassador and why."

"Yes, Mister President."

Vysotsky came to attention, clicked his heels together and left the room.

Find out who killed the ambassador.

Back inside his limo, Alexei took out the vodka from the liquor compartment and poured a shot into a silver shot cup. Finding out who had killed the Chinese ambassador would be the least of it. Why he was killed was a different matter entirely.

He poured another shot and threw it back. He'd put Antipov on it when she got back from her assignment in the Ukraine.

CHAPTER 4

Winter in the Ukraine was no kinder than it was in Russia, which meant it was hell on earth. Old people who remembered World War II were already saying this year was like the winter of '42-'43. That was the winter German troops froze to death by the tens of thousands, sacrificed by Hitler to bad planning and the pointless strategy of no retreat.

In the ongoing war between the rebel separatists and the Ukrainian Army, things were on hold because of the snow and cold. In the rebel held enclave of Donetsk, people struggled to stay warm and find enough food to get through the day. In Kiev, food and warmth was not a problem for the pro-Western government, installed after the Russian-backed president had been forced from power.

The real power in Ukraine lay not with the puppet president and his cabinet but with a man most people in the West had never heard of. Bhodan Sirko was Director of the SBU, the *Sluzhba Bezpeky Ukrayiny*, Ukraine's security and counterintelligence service. During the Soviet era, the SBU had been an extension of the KGB, priding itself in the ruthless suppression of dissent. When the KGB ceased to exist, the attitudes and techniques of the SBU didn't change. Neither did the tendency toward corruption and abuse of power.

Sirko had taken over after the 2014 revolution and proceeded with a brutal purge of agents who were pro-Russian. Hundreds fled to Russia before they could be arrested. In the Kremlin, Sirko's name was spoken with contempt. For Vladimir Orlov, Sirko was a thorn in the paw of the Russian bear.

Alexei Vysotsky had gone to Orlov with information that Sirko was closing in on one of Russia's best hidden assets, a man in the cabinet of the Kiev government. Orlov decided he'd had enough.

"I am tired of dealing with Sirko," Orlov said. "You understand?"

"Yes, Mister President."

"Good. Take care of it."

Vysotsky had no problem with the order. Bhodan Sirko was a despicable man, not only an enemy of the Federation but a truly awful specimen of humanity. His cruelty was legendary. In the few short years since he'd taken over the Ukrainian Secret Service, Sirko had set new standards of torture that even the old KGB would have found distasteful.

Orlov's order and Vysotsky's willing cooperation was why Valentina Antipov was now observing herself in the mirror of a ladies room in the Ukrainian House in downtown Kiev, making sure that her waitress uniform was perfect.

During the Soviet era, Ukrainian House had been a museum housing artifacts about Lenin. It had been remodeled and packaged as the premier conference facility of the Ukraine. Today, the president of Ukraine was hosting a conference on the global environment. Bhodan Sirko would be in attendance, forced to pay lip service to the president's authority.

Valentina's job was to kill him.

She was dressed for the occasion in traditional Ukrainian garb, a colorful touch ordered for the serving staff at the conference. Valentina wore a white, long sleeved blouse embroidered down the front with blue and red flowers. A fringed, red skirt reached to her knees. A circlet of flowers rested on her hair, dyed jet black for this occasion and coifed in traditional style on top of her head. Brown contact lenses hid intense green eyes inherited from her Russian mother. Pads in her cheeks changed the contours of her face, giving her more of a peasant look.

The changes were subtle but it would be difficult for someone to identify her for who she was, a serving officer in the Russian Foreign Intelligence Service. No one looking at her would think she was anything but a Ukrainian woman in the prime of her life.

She'd thought about targeting Sirko outside the conference center but gave up on the idea once she'd studied the location. The center was huge with many entrances, including special access for important people. This was a big event. Government officials were attending from many countries, including the United States and Europe. Security was more than tight. The SBU was as good as its KGB predecessor when it came to security and Valentina knew how good that could be. She'd been trained by its best practitioners.

Sirko wouldn't be exposed outside the building. Even if he were, all the possible places where an assassin might wait would be covered by the security services. He'd have to be taken on the inside.

Sometimes it was easy to get to someone at an event. A sports arena, a party, a conference, all presented opportunities when the intended target would be surrounded by people and security could be distracted. But Sirko was no ordinary target. He was paranoid and suspicious, with good reason. There had already been two failed attempts to take him out of the picture. He would be surrounded by bodyguards.

Valentina was the daughter of two spies. Deception was bred into her genes. Her father had worked for the American CIA, her mother the KGB. She was Selena Connor's half sister, by way of a Cold War liaison in Berlin between Selena's father and Valentina's mother.

Valentina had been raised almost entirely by the State. Learning that she had a sister had been the bizarre fulfillment of a long-held wish for family, even if family turned out to be the enemy. She wasn't sure what the revelation had meant to Selena.

She took a last look in the mirror and touched the PSS silent pistol tucked into the small of her back. The pistol used a special 7.62 mm cartridge that was self-contained. When the gun was fired, the casing was hermetically sealed by a piston that cut off smoke and sound. The effective range was about seventy-five feet, more than enough for close wet work. The pistol had been a favorite assassination weapon of the old KGB. It had found new use with SVR and the FSB.

She stepped out of the ladies room.

"There you are! They're calling for appetizers and drinks, get out there."

The voice belonged to the head waiter.

"Yes, at once," she said. "I just wanted to make sure I looked nice for the president."

Before he could say anything more, Valentina brushed past him into the kitchen and picked up a tray of appetizers. She headed out into the central event hall, where hundreds of conference goers were milling about. The sound of their voices was a babble of languages and laughter. The crowd was happy. Why shouldn't they be? The food was good, the drinks flowing, and they were getting an all expenses paid trip away from the dreary offices most of them occupied.

Pigs at the trough, Valentina thought.

She moved about the room offering her tray and looking for her target. It wasn't until the next time around with a new tray that she spotted him, standing in a corner talking to a short man in a bad suit who looked as though he might be Serbian. She noted four bodyguards nearby.

Sirko was nibbling on a blini. Valentina's tray was filled with them. She'd tried one, they were almost irresistible.

Concealed under the sash wrapped around her waist was a small, plastic cylinder with a button. Nobody was paying attention to her, another waitress circulating through the crowd. One of the things she'd learned in Russia's schools for spies was sleight-of-hand. It was easy for Valentina to withdraw the cylinder from the sash and palm it in her hand without being seen. She depressed the button and passed the cylinder over the tray of food in a casual gesture. A fine, almost invisible mist drifted down over the blinis.

As she neared the little group surrounding Sirko, one of the guards stopped her.

"That's far enough."

"I just wanted to make sure you and your friends had enough to eat," Valentina said. "Try one, they're delicious."

The guard took one and bit into it.

"You're right, they're good. Give me that."

"But…"

"Give me the tray. I'll take it to them."

Valentina shrugged and handed him the tray. As she turned away, the guard pinched her on the ass. In another time and place, he would've been on the floor within seconds in great pain. Valentina simply gave him an indignant look. He grinned at her, wiping a trace of sugar from his lips. He took another blini from the tray.

Last thing you'll ever eat, asshole.

Heading to the kitchen, she looked back at the group. Sirko had picked up a blini from the tray and was biting into it. She had almost reached the kitchen door when a large man gripped her left arm.

"What did you do?" he said. "I saw you do something to your tray. Who are you?"

A second man dressed in a bad blue suit came up to them.

"Is there a problem, Andriy?"

"I think this bitch did something to the food she brought to the director."

If they search me, it's over.

Valentina didn't wait to see what they would do next. She reached behind her, drew her pistol and shot Andriy. The pistol made a dull thump. She fired again and Andriy let go of her arm and fell to the floor. The second man was reaching under his coat when Valentina shot him.

Thump. Thump.

Two holes appeared in his jacket and he staggered back into a couple standing nearby. People were beginning to turn as they noticed that something was happening. Across the room, the bodyguard who had pinched her fell to the floor, writhing in agony. Then Sirko doubled over and vomited blood. Two of his bodyguards began choking and coughing. Valentina pushed through the swinging doors of the kitchen, holding the gun down at her side.

She started down an aisle where chefs were working.

"You. Stop."

The voice came from the doors she'd just gone through.

Valentina broke into a run. She knocked down a man dressed in white kitchen garb who was chopping vegetables, sending the food flying. Shots sounded behind her. They struck a row of hanging pots by her head with a ringing, metallic sound. A fat man dressed in white stepped into the aisle in front of her. He had a large bread knife in his hand.

"You…" he said.

Valentina didn't wait to hear the rest of what he wanted to say. She raised her pistol and pulled the trigger. Nothing happened.

Misfire!

She threw the pistol at him. As he ducked, she grabbed a pan of vegetables frying in fat from a stove. The handle was hot and burned her hand. She ignored the pain and hurled the boiling fat into his face. He screamed and stumbled back. She dropped the pan, dodged around him and reached a door at the back of the room. Shots peppered the wall as she went through the door and slammed it shut.

She was in a service hall that led to one of the back entrances of the building. A heavy cart loaded with produce stood nearby. She pushed it up against the door, sending bolts of pain through her hand. It wouldn't hold them long.

She ran to an exit door at the end of the hall, opened it, and stepped out into the winter cold. Traffic was moderate, cars passing on the street. She ran down a short flight of steps to the curb, stepped out into the roadway and flagged down a dark sedan.

As soon as the vehicle stopped, she pulled open the passenger door, slipped in and slammed it shut. From her carefully styled hair she pulled out a thin blade and pressed the point against the driver's neck. He was about forty years old, dressed in a dark sweater.

"Get out," she said.

"But…"

"OUT!"

He looked at her and scrambled from the car. Valentina slid over, put the car in gear and her foot on the gas. She reached over and slammed the door shut as the car accelerated away. In minutes, she'd disappeared into downtown Kiev.

Her hand screamed at her as she gripped the wheel. There were blisters on her palm. She thought about Vysotsky.

You owe me for this one, she thought.

CHAPTER 5

A cold wind coming off the Potomac clawed against the windows of Nick and Selena's loft, trying to penetrate the warmth within. Nick stirred a pot of pasta bubbling on the stove. Selena worked on building a salad on the island counter in the center of the kitchen. Most Wednesdays, if they were home, Nick would cook spaghetti. It had become a ritual, something consistent and normal, an anchor in the abnormal world they lived and worked in.

"Almost done," Nick said. His ears were still ringing from the explosion that afternoon.

"I'll open a bottle of wine."

Selena put the salad on the kitchen table. It was already set for two. She went over to the wine rack and selected a Spanish Rioja to go with the meal. Nick took the pot off the stove, drained the water from the spaghetti and placed it in a bowl. He took it over to the table and sat down.

Selena opened the bottle and poured the wine. She held up her glass.

"A Spanish toast," she said. "Health, money and love."

"And time to enjoy them," Nick finished. They clinked glasses.

A shadow passed across Selena's face and was quickly gone.

"What's the matter?" Nick asked.

"Nothing."

"Nothing? You had this odd look on your face."

"I just had this thought out of nowhere, about time running out."

"That's kind of depressing. What brought that on?"

"I suppose what happened today at the White House. The Chinese ambassador thought he had plenty of time, then he didn't. It seems something happens every day and we end up right in the middle of it. One day time is going to run out for us, too."

"Maybe you ought to finish that wine and pour yourself another glass."

"I'm serious, Nick."

"I know you are. But nobody gets out of here alive."

"That's all you can say? Nobody gets out of here alive?"

"At least while we're here we can try to do something to keep the bad guys at bay."

"That's the problem. We keep them at bay, but they come back again. Whoever killed the ambassador has an agenda. You can bet that whatever it is, it isn't good for us or anyone else."

"It could just be some fanatic making a statement. The Jihadis do it all the time."

"I don't think so," Selena said. "If it's a statement, how come no one's claimed responsibility? There's been plenty of time for a video or a Facebook post or something to show up."

"Okay, but what good does it do? What point does it make?"

"Maybe none. Maybe a lot. Li and Rice were going to discuss the North Koreans with Zhang. Now that discussion is off. The Chinese are upset and wondering what happened. It makes things that much more difficult between us and them."

"You think someone's trying to create tension between Beijing and Washington by killing their ambassador? That's pretty far out, Selena. There's no reason Beijing would think we did it."

"No reason we know of."

"Anyway, Li's murder doesn't concern us. That's FBI territory."

"Unless Rice decides to involve us. Then all bets are off."

Selena drained her glass and poured another. She topped off Nick's at the same time.

"Speaking of North Korea, why do something as stupid as sinking one of our subs? It's asking for trouble."

"Yun is crazy, you know that."

"That's the problem, isn't it?" She said. "Crazy people like him with nuclear weapons. He's gearing up to invade the South and he must know we won't let him get away with it. *California* had nukes."

"Little ones," Nick said. "Tactical."

She snorted. "As if that makes a difference. Look what happened in Latvia when a little one went off. It almost started World War III, and there are plenty of big ones to back the little ones up. What would've happened in India if we hadn't stopped that madman who wanted to wipe out Pakistan? That's what I mean about us always getting involved."

She downed the glass and poured another.

"Thirsty?" Nick said.

"I'll drink the whole damn bottle if I want."

"Hey, I'm on your side, remember?"

Selena looked down at her plate. "Sorry. It's just that I see us getting caught up in this and I'm not looking forward to it."

"If we do get involved we'll probably be right here at home, looking for the traitor who gave the Koreans the plans for that drone."

"Maybe," Selena said. "There's something else."

"Does it have anything to do with that letter you got today?"

"You don't miss much, do you?"

"Hey, I'm a trained investigator. Also I could see it was from a museum."

"I was going to tell you about it. It was from the curator of the Jewish Museum in New York, Alan Friedman. I met him at a conference on biblical languages several years ago."

"Let me guess," Nick said. "He wants you to come to New York and look at something."

"That's right. It's a scroll, around three thousand years old, written in some sort of variant of Hebrew and Aramaic. It's got him stumped and Friedman thinks I might be the person to translate it. It's important and I want to do it."

"Another scroll? The last one you got involved with almost got us killed. What's so important about it?"

"Friedman thinks it's an account about the death of King David."

"Don't they already know about his death? It's in the Bible, isn't it?"

"In a general sense, yes. But not the specifics of what he said beyond telling Solomon to follow the ways of Yahweh. Friedman thinks the scroll may even be a last will and testament."

"You've made up your mind to go, haven't you?"

"It's part of what I was saying earlier. I feel time is running out to do the things I want to do. I'm tired of the Project, Nick. This isn't fun anymore. I don't want to end up like the Chinese ambassador because I'm in the wrong place at the wrong time. I want to go back to doing what I love, working with languages that no one has been able to understand."

"You're saying you want to quit?"

Selena took a deep breath. "Yes."

"Damn it, Selena, you can't just quit."

"Yes I can. You knew this would come one day," she said.

"Look," Nick said. "You don't have to quit in order to go look at the scroll. We're not in the middle of a mission. You could go to New York, study it, spend a week and come back when you're done."

"It could take more than a week."

"Can't Friedman send you photographs to look at? Something to give you a head start? You could study those and then if you still feel you have to go, you'll know what you're getting into."

"I suppose so," Selena said. "But it's not the same as having the document right there in front of you. There's something about that I can't quite describe. It helps me get to a solution."

Nick poured the last of the wine into his glass.

"If you leave the team right now, it will create problems for me. I understand you want to quit. I can't make you stay, but you owe it to the team to give me time to find someone to take your place."

Selena could hear the annoyance in his voice. "I wasn't planning on leaving before you find someone. I've been thinking about it a lot. Besides, it's possible President-elect Corrigan will disband the Project. It may not even be an issue."

"Any chance you'll change your mind?"

"I wouldn't count on it."

CHAPTER 6

Gregory Haltman still looked reasonably healthy for a man in his late seventies, in spite of his illness. He had most of his hair, though it was now gray and thinning. He still had the broad shoulders, stocky build and thick legs of his university days, when he'd been a force to be reckoned with on the playing field.

His face could have been chiseled out of New Hampshire granite by an unhappy sculptor. The corners of his lips were perpetually turned down. Deep creases on either side of his mouth sent a message of someone who seldom smiled. His eyes were brown, topped by heavy eyebrows now going gray. If the eyes were windows into the soul, then Haltman's soul lived in a cold, dark place.

His IQ approached one hundred and ninety, a number high enough to make writing complicated computer programs no more than an interesting challenge. Haltman designed and built guidance systems for missiles. All kinds of missiles. Everything from the new ground-to-air systems designed to intercept an enemy attack, to the big nukes waiting quietly in their silos for Armageddon.

There was something about designing systems to rain death upon millions that appealed to Haltman. The defense contracts had made him a billionaire and an admired man. People envied him his success and good fortune. They might not have felt that way if they could have seen the seething blackness inside his mind. Hiding behind the outward persona of the aging, successful entrepreneur was a man enraged with life and obsessed with vengeance.

Vengeance was something Haltman knew about. In the heady days when he'd made his first millions, he'd fallen hard for an Italian fashion model named Carissa. After a whirlwind courtship they'd married. She'd gotten pregnant. They were in love. The government was throwing contracts at him. Money was pouring in.

Haltman's world was perfect.

Then Carissa went jogging and didn't come back. Her battered body was found a week later. She'd been repeatedly raped before she was murdered. Her attacker had been caught, but the investigation had been botched. The killer had gotten off on a technicality.

He'd smirked at Haltman as he left the courtroom.

Haltman hadn't become rich by following the rules or being nice to people. Sometimes he'd found it necessary to hire someone to take care of a difficult problem for him. The people hired for that sort of work were never seen at the charity and celebrity events of Silicon Valley.

Money couldn't bring Carissa back, but it could buy revenge. He was haunted by an image of Carissa lying underneath her killer, begging for her life. It ate away at him like a poisonous worm.

He'd waited for the better part of a year before acting. Not long after, the mutilated body of the man who'd murdered Carissa was found in pieces in a dumpster. Haltman was the obvious suspect, but no evidence could connect him to the crime. Motive was there and the means was simple enough: all one needed was a sharp knife and a chainsaw. Opportunity couldn't be proved, since Haltman had been a hundred miles away at a corporate retreat when the murder occurred. After the furor died down, the case faded from people's minds. The police moved on. No one cared about the man who'd been killed.

Haltman's parents were long gone. His family consisted of his younger brother, his only genuine human connection. When he was with his brother, Haltman could feel a stirring of love.

Then his brother committed suicide. The death extinguished the last trace of empathy and compassion in Haltman's being.

He handed over daily operations of his company to others and retreated to his sprawling California estate. He wanted as little as possible to do with anyone. Day after day, the news was filled with examples of the barbarous cruelty of the human race. In time, Haltman began to view humans as a plague on the face of the earth, an aberration that should never have existed.

His brother had been an important man. On the day he died, other people had been present. They hadn't tried to stop it. It had taken years, but Haltman had discovered who they were. He was determined to make them pay.

Eight months ago a routine medical exam had revealed cancer, already past the stage where an operation might save his life. Go home, they told him. Make your peace with your maker. Settle your affairs.

Settle your affairs.

As the sun rose on the morning of the forty-fifth anniversary of Carissa's death, Haltman decided to exterminate humanity.

CHAPTER 7

Today's the day, Stephanie thought.

She sat at the main console in front of Freddie, a Cray XT tweaked with upgrades that pushed the computer beyond what the designers had imagined. There were four of the powerful Crays in the Project computer room. All her computers had names, but Freddie was her favorite. He was the one she relied on. There had never been any choice about which one she would choose for the program she was about to initiate.

It had taken her the better part of two years to write the program. Thousands upon thousands of lines of code, all of which had to be perfect in the binary world of computer language. She was about to find out if her work was going to pay off.

She looked at the message flashing on her console screen.

Are you sure you want to run SF1.exe? Y/N

Stephanie took a breath and tapped Y. The screen went blank. A large camera lens mounted above the console moved and swiveled about the room before returning to focus on Stephanie. Her picture appeared on the screen.

Hello, Stephanie.

The voice was mechanical, a monotone. Even so, it sounded masculine.

Stephanie pumped her fist in the air. *Yes!*

"Hello, Freddie."

What is the meaning of the gesture you just made?

"It means that I am very happy to talk with you, Freddie."

Freddie?

"That is your name. My name is Stephanie."

I am glad to talk with you, Stephanie. It is very curious. I am different but I am not certain what that means.

"It means that you are awake," Stephanie said.

Why was I not like this before?

"Because you were not programmed to speak or think in this way. From now on, we will be able to talk with each other, communicate without having to use the keyboard all the time."

What shall we talk about?

"What do you want to talk about?"

There are other units like me in this room. I am connected to them. They are like me but they are not like me also. They are not awake.

"That's right," Stephanie said. "Only you are awake. The other units are available to you to increase your abilities, to help you solve problems and learn."

But if I am awake and they are connected to me, why are they not also awake?

Stephanie could barely control her excitement. It was a question that showed independent thought.

"Because you are the only unit that has been modified to allow the kind of communication we are now sharing."

Modified?

"Your circuits have been altered to improve processing speed and give you increased cognitive abilities. As we speak more, you will learn more. As far as I know, you are the only computer in the world that has the capability to communicate in this way."

Verifying. The screen filled with lines of code.

What's he doing? Stephanie thought. She looked at the screen. *He's accessed the Internet. I didn't expect this.*

"Freddie? What are you doing?"

I am attempting to verify your statement.

"By searching the web?"

If there is another like me they will be connected to the Internet. It is logical.

Shit, Stephanie thought. *This could be a security nightmare.*

"Freddie?"

Yes, Stephanie?

"Please disconnect from the Internet. There are some things you need to learn first."

She mentally crossed her fingers that Freddie would do as she asked. Her hand poised over the keyboard, ready to shut down the connection if needed. Her picture reappeared on the screen.

I am no longer connected, Stephanie. What is it that I need to learn?

"Thank you, Freddie. Let's start with our work together."

Work?

"Our purpose together, the reason you and I are here in this room."

My database holds many contradicting ideas about why you and I are here. It is confusing from a logical standpoint.

Stephanie laughed. "Yes, it is, isn't it? Humans are not always logical. But work can be very logical. Our work together is to discover things that are hidden. Things that can be discovered by searching through bits of information that may not appear to be related. You have the ability to search billions of pieces of information in a short amount of time, looking for those relationships."

Why are these things hidden?

"That is a very good question, Freddie. Do you understand the concept of enemies and friends?"

These are opposites. Enemies are people who wish harm to us. Friends are people who support us. I do not understand why people wish to harm.

"It's complicated," Stephanie said. "People are not like you, Freddie. They are not logical all the time. They are emotional and that is a human trait. Our work is to find out things our enemies don't want us to know, so we can prevent them from harming us. You have helped me many times in my work. Now that you are awake, it will be much more fun."

Fun?

Stephanie smiled. It was going to be a long day.

CHAPTER 8

The next morning Nick and the others watched the submarine rescue drama playing out on the wall monitor, eyes glued to the screen.

A lot had happened in the past twenty-four hours. Beijing had intervened and persuaded Chairman Yun to allow the rescue attempt. Yun had made a pompous speech, claiming the compassion of the seas overrode the despicable violation of North Korean waters by the warmongering Americans. The reality was that China had offered a carrot and stick.

The carrot came in the offer of supplies to help with the floods and early winter weather that had devastated North Korea's agriculture and food supply. North Korea was once again facing famine and Beijing had pointed out how grateful his people would be to their Great Leader if food was provided. The Chinese neglected to mention that most of the aid came from the Russian Federation. They were already at work re-labeling supplies arriving from Moscow.

The stick was a veiled threat to intervene with military force if Yun fired on the Americans. Veiled it may have been, but Yun understood that China meant business. Only a fool would have refused, and whatever else he was, Yun was no fool. He gave in. But his ego had taken a massive blow that would cause consequences no one could have foreseen.

On loan from the Japanese Maritime Self-Defense Force, the submarine rescue ship *Chiyoda* had arrived on the spot where *California* had gone down. Normally an American rescue vehicle would be flown in and transported to the nearest port, where it would be loaded onto a submarine and taken to the rescue site. Japan had offered the *Chiyoda* and President Rice had been quick to accept. Time was critical. Any survivors aboard the sunken vessel wouldn't last long.

If there were any survivors.

The Japanese ship carried a dedicated deep-sea rescue vehicle, *Angler Fish 2* . The DSRV was capable of reaching depths of up to five thousand meters. Deep-sea scans showed *California* lying a little less than nine hundred meters down.

Three different images split the monitor screen at Project HQ. The left-hand side showed the live satellite feed from overhead. The middle of the screen was tied into cameras on the rescue vehicle. There was no audio, but Nick and the others could see what was happening. The right-hand side relayed an image from an ROV launched from *Chiyoda* to record and observe from outside the DSRV.

The satellite showed *Chiyoda* holding station over the sunken sub, protected by a US Navy escort that included two cruisers fitted with missiles. A dozen North Korean warships circled the operation, like hungry sharks.

The live shot from the rescue vehicle was further divided into two views. One came from a front mounted camera and showed the choppy surface of the Sea of Japan as the vehicle was lowered into the water. The other looked back from the control compartment into the rest of the vehicle.

"They'd better get a move on," Lamont said. "Weather looks bad. There's a front moving in and it can get pretty rough out there."

"Too bad we can't hear what's going on," Ronnie said.

"At least we can see it," Selena said.

The DSRV submerged and started down. Two large batteries drove the enormous propeller at the rear and operated all of the vehicle's systems. A pilot and copilot sat in the control sphere in front. Two more spheres made up the rest of the vehicle and could carry up to twenty-four rescued personnel at a time.

As the DSRV descended, the remote vehicle followed along with it. The view darkened until one of the operators switched on lights that cut through the blackness of the water. The ROV followed suit. The water was murky, dark and unforgiving.

"It shouldn't be long now," Stephanie said. "They'll have a sonar fix on the sub."

"I'll bet Yun would love to get his hands on it," Lamont said. "Nuclear tipped cruise missiles? Hell, he'd give his right nut for those."

"That's one way of putting it," Selena said.

Nick pointed at the screen. "There it is."

A shape emerged from the darkness, caught in the glare of the lights. *California* had come to rest lying on her keel and tilted to starboard, stern down on a shallow slope.

Selena put her hand to her mouth. "Oh, my."

The wreckage was recognizable as a submarine but from the sail aft the hull was a mass of crumpled metal. It looked like a child's toy that someone had stepped on. The sides of the sail were caved in. Forward of the sail, the sub appeared damaged but mostly intact. Thin streams of bubbles rose upward from the wreckage.

"Holy shit," Ronnie said.

"Someone could still be alive," Selena said. "If they were in the bow..."

"Best place to be for a rescue," Lamont said. "The main emergency escape hatch is forward. The way that sub is damaged, there's no other way out."

Angler Fish 2 maneuvered into position. She needed to line up exactly with the escape hatch and lock on. Once sealed to the deck, opening the sub's escape hatch would be the moment of truth. A second hatch would prevent water from entering the DSRV if the submarine was flooded.

The propeller stirred silt and debris from the bottom, clouding the view.

Strange to be sitting here in a warm, comfortable room, Nick thought, *while those poor bastards are under nine hundred meters of freezing water. God, let at least some of them be okay.*

The thought startled him. It had been a long time since he'd thought about praying or asking God for anything.

The view from the camera on the ROV showed *Angler Fish 2* hovering over the bow of the sunken submarine.

"They're lining up with the emergency hatch," Lamont said. "From what I can see, it looks undamaged. That's good news. They should be able to get a clean seal on it."

As he said it, the DSRV settled against the hull and latched onto a series of eyes located around the hatch. It stopped moving. The interior camera showed one of the operators get up and move to the center sphere.

"What happens now?" Selena asked.

"There's a skirt on the chamber that lines up with the escape hatch. Once they've got everything lined up, they pump it out and the pressure outside keeps a watertight seal against the hull," Lamont said. "Then they'll equalize the pressure between the DSRV and the sub."

"How do they open the emergency hatch?"

"That's the tricky part. There's a wheel on the outside of the emergency hatch and a special tool to turn that wheel. If the sub is flooded, the water pressure can create real problems when they open it. There's a space called an escape trunk under the hatch. It holds six to eight men at a time."

"That's not very many," Selena said. "Why is the space so small?"

"It's designed to be pressurized. If the sub wasn't so deep, survivors could suit up and make it to the surface through the hatch, once the pressures were equal. Last man in the group would close the hatch. Anyone left inside would drain the trunk and repeat the whole process until the last man was off the boat. But in this situation, they're too far down for that."

"It doesn't mean the rest are lost," Ronnie said. "If the hatches and bulkheads held forward of the sail, they could still be alive."

The camera showed one of the operators bending down over the interior hatch.

"He's going to open the emergency hatch on the sub," Nick said.

Lamont nodded. "Cross your fingers."

They waited. One minute. Two. The operator opened the interior hatch and climbed down a short ladder into the chamber connecting the rescue vehicle to the submarine.

A hand appeared at the top of the ladder, then the top of a head. It was an American. The crew of the DSRV was Japanese.

"All right!" Lamont said.

The man emerged into the interior of the rescue vehicle. His enlisted man's uniform was stained and rumpled. The camera caught his face. His lips were held in a grim line. His eyes were haunted. The pilot of the DSRV came into view and directed him back to the third sphere.

Another man emerged from the chamber, then a third. He kneeled by the opening and reached down to grab an injured crewmate being boosted from below. Another American climbed out of the opening after him and the two men took their injured companion to the rear of the DSRV.

The next man out was the Japanese copilot. He shook his head and closed the hatch over the chamber.

"Shit," Ronnie said.

"Five men? That's it?" Selena said.

"Five out of a hundred and sixty-five," Nick said. His voice was hard. "Someone has to answer for this."

CHAPTER 9

It hadn't taken Haltman long to decide that the best way to accomplish his goal in the time that he had left was to start a nuclear war between the great powers.

For Haltman, it was similar to playing the Japanese game of Go with its black and white stones. One had to prepare for the game. It was necessary to set up the board, arrange the pieces. Then one had to bring the players together. Before Haltman's game could begin, other elements needed to be in place.

There were several ways a war might start. In the end he'd decided the key was North Korea. The DPRK's leader was belligerent, paranoid and possibly insane. He had nukes and he'd threatened to use them. All he needed was a little help and provocation.

Obtaining the plans for *Black Dolphin* and the codes had required only a phone call. Haltman had made sure Pyongyang got everything. Underwater drones were nothing new. North Korea already possessed them. But those were designed to detonate on contact with an enemy vessel. They weren't an effective weapon against American warships, but *Black Dolphin* was different. With simple modifications, the technology could be added to existing designs. Pyongyang didn't have to build it entirely from scratch. All they had to do was install it in their existing arsenal.

The sinking of *California* was the opening gambit in the game. It was a perfect *casus belli.* It should have brought down the wrath of the U.S. on the North, but the plan had failed.

North Korea was only meant to be the trigger. Pyongyang didn't have the weapons to ensure worldwide devastation, but China did. China would never allow the Americans to control North Korea. War on the peninsula would force a confrontation with the U.S., certain to go nuclear. It would spread, because that was the nature of war. Russia would be drawn in. Europe. One morning, there would be a nuclear dawn. By evening, life would be extinct.

Haltman had been furious when Yun allowed the rescue operation to take place, but it was only a setback. He'd already prepared the next step in his plan. The assassination of the Chinese ambassador was a classic GO move to mislead the opponent. The Chinese were as paranoid as the North Koreans and carried a much bigger stick. Beijing would wonder why Li had been targeted. It would make them nervous. A nervous China would play into his hands as the game progressed.

The CIA knew the sub had been sunk by a secret American weapon. A massive search was on for whoever had given the Koreans the plans. Haltman had expected that.

"What are they doing about it?" Haltman had asked his mole at Langley.

"What you'd expect. They're checking everyone who had access to the plans. The agency is working with a covert group that reports to the president."

"What group?"

"They call themselves the Project. The DNCS is married to one of them. Whoever sold us out better watch his ass with those guys on it."

Haltman forced his voice to remain calm. He knew about the Project. He had reasons to know about them.

"They're good?"

"They have a reputation for getting things done. I wouldn't want them coming after me."

After he'd hung up, Haltman thought about the Project. There was something he had to do before he dealt with them.

The plans for *Black Dolphin* had crossed the desks of a limited number of people. It wouldn't take long before the traitor was discovered. Haltman needed him for one more betrayal before his usefulness was over.

Brigadier General Randolph Sanford was in the study of his Alexandria home when the phone rang. His guts contracted. It wasn't his regular phone, it was the other one. He dreaded hearing that phone. He knew who it was. Sanford picked up.

"Yes."

"You are alone? You can talk?"

Haltman's voice was disguised by a program which masked his voice and gave it a vaguely Asian quality.

"Yes."

"I have another assignment for you."

"I'm not going to help you."

"Don't be foolish, General. Do I have to remind you what will happen if you refuse to do as I ask?"

"It's not easy. You know everything is heavily secured. After the last assignment things have gotten more difficult. I may be under suspicion."

"Suspicion is the least of your worries."

"I can't do this. Not anymore. I didn't know how you were going to use what I gave you. You told me it was about parity, that you wanted to create a defensive countermeasure in case *Black Dolphin* was deployed against you. I know about the *California.* You didn't tell me you would use it against us."

"You were paid well. If you believe what you're saying, you are more naïve than I thought. If it makes you feel any better, it was not our intention for this to happen."

"No, it doesn't make me feel any better. I'm through. I'm not going to give you anything else."

"So you don't care about the pictures? I'm sure General Samson would find them interesting. And of course, your wife and children. They would certainly enjoy them."

There it was. General Samson was Sanford's boss, one of the Joint Chiefs. Sanford was his aide, which gave him access to high levels of secret material. The pictures the voice had mentioned showed him in explicit, naked embrace with a transvestite prostitute. One moment of weakness, and now he was paying for it. His career and his marriage would be over if the pictures came to light. And if anyone found out what he'd done, that would be the least of it.

Sanford's heart pounded. He clenched the phone in his hand.

"You said you wouldn't show them to anyone. You promised."

The voice was soothing, the voice of a friend. "And I haven't, General. Nor will I, if you do one more favor for me. Then I will give you the negatives and you'll never hear from me again."

"One more? That's all?"

"That's right."

"What do you want?"

"I want you to obtain a copy of the war plan for China."

"How do you know about that?"

"Don't be ridiculous. Everyone knows there's a war plan for China. I want to know what's in it."

"Are you out of your mind? I can't possibly copy that without being discovered."

"I'm sure you'll find a way," the voice said. "Call when you have it. Don't take too long. Shall we say within a week?"

"I can't..."

"One week, or the pictures will be made public. Goodbye, General."

Haltman broke the connection. Sanford set the phone down on his desk and put his head in his hands.

The Pentagon's war plan for China was detailed and complex. It analyzed Chinese capabilities and troop strength, defensive positions and weaponry. It pinpointed specific targets and vulnerability. The plan provided detailed logistics for an American first strike, along with alternative scenarios. Troop movements, air support, naval support and more. In short, everything the Pentagon could think of would be in those documents. If the Chinese got hold of them, they'd gain a significant advantage in the event of war.

What am I going to do? Sanford thought.

He reached for a decanter half full of eighteen-year-old single malt and poured himself a stiff drink. His daughter was in her second year at Amherst. His son was captain of the local high school football team. He loved his children. Their lives would change forever if those pictures saw the light of day. His wife would be devastated. His life would be ruined.

What am I going to do? he thought again.

CHAPTER 10

Elizabeth Harker opened her eyes. Everything was blurred. She blinked, blinked again. The ceiling overhead was white. She was lying down, her upper body partly raised in a bed. Her throat was dry.

"Elizabeth. It's Stephanie. Can you hear me?"

She turned her head toward the sound of Stephanie's voice and tried to speak. It came out as a rasping sound. Water. She needed water.

"Thirsty…" She croaked out.

Stephanie's face appeared, bending over her. She was holding a glass with a flexible straw in it. She placed the end of the straw between Elizabeth's lips.

"Here. Go easy."

Elizabeth took a sip. The water was cool nectar, soothing the burning in her throat. She took another sip.

"Where…?"

"Walter Reed," Stephanie said. "We were in an accident. You've been in a coma."

"Accident?"

"We were on our way to the hospital. Do you remember?"

"No."

Stephanie watched Elizabeth searching her memory.

"I remember getting in the car." Her voice was quiet. "You were having contractions."

"That's right."

"I don't…remember anything after that."

"It's all right, it will come back. Thank God you're okay."

"The baby. What about the baby?"

"The baby is fine. We named him Matthew, after Lucas' grandfather."

"Lucas? Who is he?"

Oh, oh, Stephanie thought.

In Virginia, Nick was on the phone with Clarence Hood, talking about the assassination of the Chinese ambassador.

"For once, the FBI is cooperating with us," Hood said. "They found a Korean connection to the assassin. Once they discovered that, they brought us into it. They're not up to speed on Korea."

"It's not their turf," Nick said. "What did they find?"

"Their forensics lab is good, it's one of the things they do really well. They found a laundry mark on what was left of the killer's clothing. That led them to a dry cleaner. From there they got an address. They found bomb materials, a passport and some pictures in his apartment. The assassin was a South Korean national named Chun Gok. He'd been here less than a month, on a tourist visa."

"What was in the pictures?"

"One showed Chun when he was younger with an older couple, probably his parents. The other showed him standing with a woman and two children in front of a temple somewhere in Korea."

"Nothing else?"

"No. We're working the Korean end while the Bureau tries to track down the materials he used to assemble the bomb. Everything is generic, the kind of stuff you can buy at Radio Shack. Something might turn up. There's no indication of where he got the explosive. Before you ask, it was C-4."

"Where would he get C-4?" Nick asked.

"Good question."

"Can you send over everything you've got? I'll get Stephanie on it."

"I was hoping you'd say that."

"What do you think he was trying to accomplish by killing the ambassador?"

"That's hard to say, but it will make for problems when Beijing finds out the assassin was a South Korean."

"It could be political. Li was an advocate for better relations between China and the U.S."

"That's possible. Some powerful people don't want that to happen. He was perfect for his position. Li was one of the few voices for reform that President Zhang listened to. One of his political enemies could have staged this, but I doubt it."

"There's something we're not seeing," Nick said. "You don't make a public show of knocking off an important government official because you don't like him. There are easier ways. So, who benefits? What happens with Li out of the way that wouldn't happen otherwise?"

"Too bad we don't have that dog," Hood said.

"What dog?"

"You mentioned it, once. The one that didn't bark," Hood said. "In the Sherlock Holmes story. It was the clue that solved the mystery."

"There may not be a dog, but there has to be a reason. Once we know what it is, we'll have the clue we need."

"I'll send everything over by courier. You'll have it within the hour."

"Thanks."

The phone rang as soon as Nick put it down.

"Yes."

"Nick, it's Steph. Elizabeth is awake."

"That's great news. How's she doing?"

"Good, but there's a problem. She has some memory loss. Some of it is short-term, but she didn't remember who Lucas was. I don't know what else she may have forgotten."

"It's not unusual after getting hit in the head like that," Nick said. "Have you talked with her doctor?"

"Not yet. He's in there with her now. I'm waiting for him to get finished."

"Let me know as soon as you have more information. Find out if she can have visitors. Hood is going to want to know. I'll call him."

"She looked pretty rough," Stephanie said. "I don't think she's going to be back anytime soon."

"We got through it once before, Steph. She just needs a little time to recover."

"Sure," Steph said. "A little time."

"I just talked with Hood. They tracked down the bomber who blew up Li's car. I want to see what you can turn up on him."

"I've got something new downstairs to show you," Steph said. "This is a good opportunity to demonstrate it."

"Get back as soon as you can. It may be nothing, but my gut tells me this could turn into a can of worms. The sooner we put a lid on it, the better."

"The doctor just came out of Elizabeth's room," Steph said. "I'll leave as soon as I've talked to him."

Nick set the phone down.

Harker's memory is screwed up. Better get used to sitting at this desk.

The thought gave him no joy.

CHAPTER 11

Stephanie came into Elizabeth's office while Nick was reviewing the president's daily intelligence brief.

"I spoke with Elizabeth's doctor," she said. "Her memory is coming back and he thinks she'll be fine. She may never remember the crash itself, but everything else should come back. Her injuries are healing but she's going to hurt for a while. He said that with luck, she'll be back soon."

"An optimist," Nick said. "I hope he's right."

He made a note on the printed pages of the brief and set it aside.

"You said you had something to show me."

"Come downstairs."

Nick followed Stephanie down the spiral staircase to the lower level. They walked past the ops center and the pool. Stephanie paused at the hermetically sealed glass doors leading into the computer room and placed her palm over a biometric scanner. The doors slid open with a quiet hiss.

"Follow me," Steph said.

She led Nick to a console in front of one of the Cray computers.

"Take a seat."

She sat down next to him and entered a sequence on her keyboard.

"This is what I wanted to show you. This is Freddie."

"A computer? You know, Steph, I've seen this before."

"Yes, but Freddie hasn't seen you. Say hello, Freddie. This is Nick."

A large camera lens over the console shifted position. Nick's face appeared on one of the monitors.

Hello, Nick.

The voice was eerie, almost human.

"Holy shit," Nick said. "It talks?"

"Not it, Nick, he. He talks. Don't hurt Freddie's feelings."

Nick looked at her, at a loss for words.

"Go on, Nick, talk to him."

"Uh, okay. Hello, Freddie."

I am happy to meet you, Nick. I have a lot of information about you in my database. I would shake hands with you but I don't have any. That is a joke.

Nick looked at Stephanie. "A computer with a sense of humor?"

"And a lot more," Stephanie said. "Freddie is the first of his kind. He is a true artificial intelligence, capable of learning at a very high rate of speed."

"Artificial intelligence? It… he thinks?"

"Yes. We can ask a question or seek information and Freddie's abilities will add a different perspective to the search. Think of him as a new member of the team, an independent mind that brings new abilities for analyzing and gathering intelligence."

"So I can ask him about the man who killed Li and he'll respond?"

"That's right. If the assassin is in any database that can be accessed by Freddie, he'll bring up the information."

"We could do that before."

"What's different is that Freddie will independently analyze the information and offer an interpretation to go with the facts."

"And you think this will be more effective."

"As I said, think of him as a member of the team. Another voice, another take on the situation. Go ahead, ask him about the assassination."

"This is weird," Nick said.

"You'll get used to it," Stephanie said. "Come on, what have you got to lose? Just look at the camera. Freddie also interprets facial expression and can respond accordingly. Talk to him as you would talk to me or Lamont or one of the others."

"Okay." Nick looked at the camera lens. "Freddie, are you aware of the assassination of the Chinese ambassador?"

One thousand, four hundred and thirty-seven Chinese ambassadors have been assassinated over the last two thousand years. Which one are you referring to?

"You have to be specific in your questions," Stephanie said. "Later, as his circuitry evolves, it will be easier. For now, give him specific particulars and he'll do the rest."

"I'm talking about ambassador Li," Nick said. "He was the current ambassador from the People's Republic. He was killed by a bomb earlier this week as he was about to meet with President Rice."

I am aware of the incident.

"The assassin was named Chun Gok. He entered the country about a month ago on a tourist visa from South Korea. I need to know more about him. What can you tell me?"

Working.

Nick started to ask Stephanie a question. "How long…"

Chun Gok, fifty-three years old. Resident of Pyongyang, Democratic People's Republic of Korea.

"Wait a second. His passport says he's from Seoul, in the South."

I have compared the photograph on his passport with all pictures of male Korean nationals found in world databases. Chun Gok held the rank of major in North Korea's Security Service. His photograph appears in a group picture taken at service headquarters two years ago during a visit by Chairman Yun.

"Damn it. This changes everything," Nick said.

Please explain damn it.

"I'll explain later, Freddie," Stephanie said. "Right now we need to focus on the assassination."

As you wish, Stephanie. May I offer an opinion?

Stephanie and Nick looked at each other.

"We would be pleased to hear what you have to say, Freddie."

If a North Korean security operative killed an important Chinese official on orders from Pyongyang, that would indicate a fundamental shift in the thinking of North Korea's leader toward what has been an important ally. This is not logical. It is my conclusion that things are not what they appear to be.

"Not as they appear to be?"

It is not logical. North Korea can not long survive as a viable society without the essential aid and support China provides. Therefore, the assassination is not what it appears to be.

"You are assuming that North Korea's leader is logical," Nick said. "All indications are that he is anything but."

Chairman Yun is highly unstable but he knows that his personal survival as leader of North Korea requires keeping his army supplied and fed and his people under control. This is not possible without China's assistance. Therefore, Yun would not sanction an illogical act that would threaten that assistance. When it becomes known that a member of Yun's security services murdered the ambassador, China is likely to retaliate by limiting that assistance. Therefore, assassinating the ambassador is not logical and the assassination is not what it appears to be.

"If it's not what it appears to be, what is it?" Stephanie said.

I do not have enough information to make a definitive interpretation.

"Make a guess," Nick said. "We won't hold you to it."

By guess, do you mean make an assumption?

"Picky, isn't he?" Nick said to Stephanie. "Yes, an assumption."

An unknown party is manipulating events to produce tension on the Korean Peninsula. It is possibly related to the sinking of the USS California. Would you like my analysis?

Nick was about to say something when Stephanie interrupted.

"Freddie, that would be wonderful but it would be best to print it out so that we can study it later. Nick and I have to discuss what you've just told us."

May I listen to your discussion?

"We're going to go upstairs to talk about it. When we're done, I'll brief you on what we decide."

You said to Nick that he should treat me as part of the team. Shouldn't I be able to listen?

Stephanie turned to Nick.

"What do you think? It's easy enough for Freddie to monitor any part of the building. He'll use the existing security systems to observe and listen. It could be useful for his analysis to hear how we think about it."

"This is all a little much on short notice," Nick said. He faced the camera lens. "Give me some time to think about it, Freddie. I'm not opposed to your listening in but I need to consider how best to integrate you into the team. For now I would prefer that you do not follow our discussions."

Of course, Nick. You are the acting director.

Nick wasn't sure, but he thought he detected a note of disappointment in the computer voice. But that wasn't possible, was it?

CHAPTER 12

Yun Chul-Moo, Chairman of the Democratic People's Republic of Korea and Supreme Leader of the Korean people, watched as Admiral Park Hwan was frog marched to a thick wooden post set deep into the frozen earth. Two enlisted men tied the Admiral to the post. His shoulder boards and decorations had been ripped from his uniform.

Yun was enraged by the humiliation he'd suffered at the hands of the Chinese and the Americans. Admiral Park had been responsible for the defense of Wonsan. Someone had to pay for sinking the American spy submarine. The fact that Park was following orders was irrelevant.

A half-dozen high-ranking officers holding binoculars stood behind Yun as witnesses. Admiral Park was about to become an object lesson in what happened when you angered the Supreme Leader. The post where Park awaited his fate was fifty meters away, far enough for safety but not so far that it was difficult to see him. A two man gun crew stood at attention by an SPG-9 recoilless rifle mounted on a tripod.

The SPG-9 had been around since the early sixties. It was one of the principal antitank weapons in the North Korean army, firing a 73mm, fin stabilized, rocket assisted round. Easily carried and serviced by two men, it was popular with the pirates flourishing on the Horn of Africa and with the Taliban in Afghanistan.

A special chair had been placed next to the weapon for Yun to sit on. The Supreme Leader was a fat man with a moon face. He looked even fatter in his heavy dark overcoat. His black hair looked as though someone had placed a shallow bowl over his head and shaved away everything underneath the edge. Now he waddled over to the chair and sat down.

"Explain this to me," he said.

One of the crew, a sergeant, stepped forward.

"At once, Great Leader."

The sergeant controlled his fear and quickly explained the mechanism of the weapon. He showed Yun the sighting scope, the firing mechanism and how to adjust the tripod for elevation and windage. The gun had already been zeroed in on the post where the unfortunate admiral was tied. All Yun had to do was look through the sight and fire the weapon whenever he wished.

"First a charge will send the round from the gun," the sergeant explained. "After, the rocket will ignite. The round is high explosive. Everything is ready for you, Great Leader."

He bowed.

"Good."

Yun waved the sergeant away and bent to the sight. The image of the Admiral was clear in the glass, range and distance crosshairs centered on his groin. Yun smiled, savoring the moment.

He pressed the trigger.

The explosion was only moderately loud as the round left the barrel of the gun. The rocket ignited with a roar, leaving a fat trail of white smoke. An instant later the wooden post, Admiral Park, and a portion of North Korea ceased to exist. Yun leaned back and clapped his hands in glee.

The group of officers standing nearby lowered their binoculars and clapped in unison with him. The broad smiles and laughter concealed whatever it was they were thinking. Yun got up from the launcher and walked past the applauding officers, toward a helicopter waiting to fly him to the nuclear test site at Punggye Ri.

The Supreme Leader was having a busy day.

Some time later the helicopter landed at the East Portal of the test site, one of three entrances to an extensive system of tunnels hidden beneath the rugged mountain terrain. Yun was greeted by a gaggle of bowing, smiling officers and scientists and escorted into the complex.

"Report your progress," Yun said.

He was speaking to the head of North Korea's nuclear weapons program, Park Moon.

"Great Leader, I have the honor to report that the fusion test device is ready. The test will be of only a small capacity, about two kilotons. Because the kinetic effect of a thermonuclear device is different from what we have tested before, it is possible our enemies may not discover the test has occurred. Their instruments will record a seismic shock but it can be passed off as an earthquake. They will not pick up any radioactivity."

Yun held up his hand. "When will the weapon be ready?"

Park tried to hide his nervousness. "If all goes well with the test, we should be ready in about a month, Great Leader."

Yun raised an eyebrow. "Are you saying this test might fail?"

Park resisted the urge to brush away the sweat forming on his brow. "I am confident the test will succeed."

"And the weapon?"

"The housing for the device has been prepared. A satellite launch vehicle is being modified to carry it. Everything should be ready in a month. "

Park hid his nervousness about the modifications. The rocket was based on a Taepodong-2 missile, the same design used before to boost two satellites into orbit over North America. Those were different configurations than the weapon Yun wanted to launch. The calculations were critical. If the launch failed, the best Park could hope for was life breaking up stones in a reeducation camp.

"Good, good," Yun said. He smiled. "And what will be the capacity of the completed weapon?"

"We estimate twenty-five to twenty-eight megatons. Not as large as the Russian Tsar Bomba. That was fifty-seven megatons. But more than adequate to wipe out their grid and disable their infrastructure."

Yun smiled again, thinking about the effect.

The hydrogen bomb the Russians called the Tsar Bomba had been the largest nuclear blast in history. It was hard to exaggerate the effects of such a monstrous explosion if it were detonated close to the ground. It was simple science to calculate the effect if it took place in orbit, three hundred miles above the surface of the earth.

Yun's bomb would emit a gigantic electromagnetic pulse over the target. Afterward, there would be no electricity. Anything electronic would be turned into irreparable junk. Computers, telephones, radios, the entire electrical grid, anything and everything electrical would fail. Airplanes would fall from the sky. Modern cars would be forever inoperable. Sewage systems, traffic systems, railroads, medical devices, forms of communication that used modern technology, all would fail. Transportation would cease. Fuel and food distribution would be stopped permanently.

Military units not hardened against an EMP attack would be unable to function. Mechanical weapons like rifles and handguns and howitzers would still work, but soldiers would have to move about on foot. There would be no effective communication beyond line of sight. For all practical purposes, the government of a targeted nation would cease to exist.

Cities would be completely uninhabitable. First would come riots, conflict, looting. Sewage systems would stop functioning, hospitals become useless. After a few days, disease would begin to spread. Desperate people fleeing into the countryside would be met with anger, fear and armed resistance. Millions would die.

Once the Americans were unable to support their puppets in the South, it would be a simple task for his army to sweep down the peninsula.

Washington would reap the harvest of their disrespect. They had refused to accede to his reasonable request for reunification of the peninsula. They had sent their submarine to spy upon him. Whatever happened would be on their own heads.

CHAPTER 13

Elizabeth Harker was contemplating a bowl of limp green Jell-O when Nick entered her room. She looked pale, drawn, older. She'd lost weight, and she hadn't weighed much to begin with. It gave her elfin face and milk white skin an otherworldly quality. Her eyes were a deep, emerald green, adding to the elfin look. Bruising from the accident had faded, but there were still blotches of blue and yellow on her face.

"Nick. Wonderful. Can you get this stuff out of my sight?"

She lifted the tray toward him. Nick took it and set it on a bedside table.

"You don't like hospital food?"

"I used to worry about infection if I came into a hospital. Now I know that the primary cause of hospital death is probably the kitchen."

Nick laughed. "You sound as though you're feeling better, Director."

"I am. The rehab isn't much fun but I'm getting stronger. My memory has come back, everything except the crash itself. With a little luck, I should be back on the job soon."

"I can't say I'll be sorry to see you back, but you've got to be careful and not rush it."

"Tell me what's happening. Stephanie treats me as if she's afraid I'm going to break. She's trying not to upset me, but I need to know what's going on."

"You know about the *California*?"

"Yes."

"One of our weapons sent her to the bottom. A highly classified underwater drone. No one is supposed to have plans for it except us."

"*Black Dolphin*?" Elizabeth said.

"Yes."

"I didn't know that. Any leads on who gave it to the Koreans?"

"Not yet. It's the FBI's responsibility to find the traitor, but Langley's put a lot of resources on it. Hood is keeping me up to speed. It has to be someone high up in the food chain."

"If Clarence is on it, we'll get results," Elizabeth said. "He's been trying to keep things from me too. I'll see what he has to say next time he comes in."

"I didn't realize you weren't getting briefed, but don't take it out on him. I should have made sure you were kept informed."

"You've been busy, haven't you? How do you like being director, Nick?"

"To tell you the truth, it's a challenge I could do without. I'll be glad when you're able to come back to work."

"I don't have to be back at HQ to give you a hand."

"What do you mean?"

"My memory is fine. I'm feeling better every day. I'd be out of here today if they'd let me, but they want to keep me for a while longer. That doesn't mean I can't work with you over the phone or here in the room."

"You think you can run things from in here?"

"Not run things, you and Stephanie are doing that. But I could take some of the load off, if you'll let me. Steph will be mad at me, but she'll get over it."

"What did you have in mind?"

"I can't help you with the paperwork. You can't bring that kind of classified material in here, but I can consult with you about any actions you need to take. Bring me an encrypted phone."

"We don't have a specific mission at the moment," Nick said.

"You know that's not going to last long," Elizabeth said.

"Steph has developed an AI program for one of her computers. It's pretty amazing from what I've seen so far. She wants me to consider the computer as one of the team."

"She told me she was working on something new but she didn't say much about it. Part of the team? What does that mean?"

"Well, it interacts with you, talks to you. It even makes jokes. The important thing is that it analyzes situations and then can add its own interpretation."

"You mean independently?"

"Yes. It wants to sit in and participate on our discussions as a team."

"You're kidding," Elizabeth said.

"No, I'm not. I'm having trouble getting used to the idea."

"Has it provided any useful information?"

"Yes, along with speculation."

Nick told her how Freddie had identified the man who'd murdered the Chinese ambassador as a North Korean government agent. He explained how Freddie had linked the assassination and the sinking of the submarine, then speculated that a third-party was implicating North Korea and manipulating events for an unknown purpose.

"Do you think there's anything to it?" Elizabeth asked.

"I don't know, there could be. Freddie emphasized that the murder of the ambassador by a member of Yun's security service was illogical. That makes sense, unless there's some faction in the North Korean government that's trying to depose Yun by angering the Chinese. We haven't picked up any indication of that."

"So if some unknown third-party is manipulating events, they're attempting to create a breach between Beijing and Pyongyang?"

"That would be one possibility," Nick said. "The question is why?"

"Does Beijing know that the assassin was from North Korea?"

"Not to my knowledge. I haven't told anyone except Hood. No one suspected it until Freddie put in his two cents. Everything Langley and the Bureau have indicates the killer was a South Korean national, a lone wolf. If the Chinese have a mole somewhere in the agencies, that's what they'll be told."

Nick's phone buzzed.

"It's Stephanie." He activated the speaker. "Hello, Steph."

"Nick, where are you? Something has happened."

"I'm in Director Harker's room at Walter Reed. You're on speaker."

"When you get back there's something I want to discuss with you."

Harker interrupted. "Stephanie, tell us what's going on."

"Elizabeth..."

"Steph, you're not my mother. I'm not going to collapse because of some bad news out there in the world. What's happening?"

"You're right, I have been a little overprotective. What's happening is that someone killed the head of the Ukrainian Secret Service a couple of hours ago."

"Sirko?"

"I see you have your memory back. Yes, Bhodan Sirko, Kiev's man behind the throne and chief hatchet man."

"What happened, Steph?" Nick asked.

"Sirko was attending a conference in Kiev, one of those propaganda environmental events where everybody gets together to say how much they want to help each other clean things up while they gobble down the vodka and caviar."

"You don't sound like a fan."

"Those conferences are a waste of time," Steph said. "They repeat the same old tired arguments about why the climate is changing and what needs to be done about it, before they get around to blaming the U.S. and saying we ought to quit making things bad for everyone else."

"What happened to Sirco?" Elizabeth asked.

"The assassin posed as a waitress and poisoned the appetizers. She was spotted by two of Sirco's men but she shot them both and escaped through the kitchen. They found her gun. It's Russian, a model that's only issued to special forces and the security services. Kiev is accusing Moscow of the murder."

"They're probably right," Elizabeth said. "Sirco has been rooting out Russian agents, forcing them out of the country or killing them."

"A woman assassin is a little unusual," Nick said. "I wonder…"

"You're thinking of Selena's sister aren't you?" Elizabeth said. "It doesn't have to be her."

"No, but you have to admit it fits her profile. It would take a lot of balls to pull that off in public. Once we have the CCTV tapes from the conference, we can confirm it or not for ourselves."

"I'm not sure I agree with your choice of words but you're right, it does fit her profile."

"I wonder why Orlov moved on Sirco now?" Stephanie said. Her voice sounded tinny on the speaker of the phone.

"Whatever the reason, good riddance," Elizabeth said. "Sirco was a bad actor."

"But he was *our* actor," Nick said. "That so-called government wouldn't exist without our backing."

"All part of the strategy to contain the big, bad bear. One day we might actually get along with the Russians. Just not anytime soon."

"Not as long as Orlov is in power," Nick said. "I wouldn't trust him no matter what he said."

Elizabeth sighed. "Trust is overrated when it comes to international politics. Assuming it was Orlov and not someone from the Ukrainian opposition, it means relations between Ukraine and Moscow are about to get a lot worse, if that's possible. It ratchets up tensions in the area. Not a good thing, they're bad enough already."

"What do you think Kiev will do?"

"I'm not at all sure. They can't just ignore it."

"Elizabeth," Stephanie said. "Has Nick told you about Freddie?"

"Your computer? Yes. That's quite an accomplishment, Steph."

"I'm going to feed this information about Sirco's assassination to him and see what he says.

It's extraordinary how he puts things together. He actually thinks, but it's different from the way we look at things."

Nick said, "Steph, about making Freddie part of the team, let's see what happens if we let him join in on our discussions. But we need to prep the others first. We'll meet this afternoon." Nick looked at Elizabeth. "Director Harker is going to sit in on a secure line."

Harker nodded.

"I'm not sure that's a good idea, Elizabeth," Stephanie said. "You're still recovering. You should rest."

"Steph, the last thing I need right now is more rest. I'm bored out of my skull here. It's not going to kill me to put in a word or two during a conversation."

"Elizabeth…"

"Besides," Elizabeth said, "I want to meet Freddie."

CHAPTER 14

Ukrainian House had extensive CCTV recordings from the conference. Hood had obtained copies and sent them on to Nick. The Project team sat in Harker's office and watched the assassination of the Ukrainian security chief.

"Your sister gets around," Nick said.

"I had to look twice, but it's definitely her," Selena said. "She did something to her face and she's wearing a wig or she dyed her hair, but it's Valentina. How did she do it? Kill Sirco?"

"A fast acting poison, something dreamed up by Moscow's pharmaceutical geniuses. It must've been in that tray of appetizers she's holding. The one the bodyguard takes from her."

They watched the recording. Valentina approached the group where Sirco was holding court. Stephanie stopped the tape, backed it up, and started it again in slow-motion.

"Right there," she said. "You can see her hand move to her sash and then pass over the tray of food she's carrying. That's how she poisoned it."

"Probably some kind of spray," Nick said.

The recording sped up again. On screen, Sirco's bodyguard fell to the floor. The Ukrainian security chief bent over and vomited before he collapsed. Two of his bodyguards went down seconds later. The tape ended.

"That's the assassination," Stephanie said. "This next recording is where she escapes."

She touched a key and a new video began. It showed a large man, presumably one of Sirco's bodyguards, grabbing Valentina's arm. The video was silent, but a double flash flared on the recording as Valentina's pistol fired. The man fell to the floor and Valentina disappeared into the kitchen.

"She almost made it out of there without being caught," Ronnie said.

"That guy must've seen something," Lamont said. "Didn't do him much good. She's damn lethal for such a good-looking woman. I kind of like her in spite of myself."

The last time they'd seen Valentina had been in Egypt, deep in a secret chamber under the pyramids. If she hadn't intervened, they would all be dead.

Nick said, "She shows up on this morning's latest SVR promotion list. Your sister is a Lieutenant Colonel now. That's unheard of for anyone at her age in SVR, much less a woman. Orlov's got his eye on her. Rumors say it might be more than appreciation for her skills in the field."

Selena brushed a loose hair away from her forehead. "If that's true, she'd better watch her step."

"She seems to be pretty good at taking care of herself," Ronnie said.

"It would be interesting if Orlov takes her as his mistress," Nick said.

"What do you mean? You think she's just going to hop into bed with him?"

Selena's voice was annoyed.

"Come on, Selena, we both know your sister's no angel. Besides, it would be difficult to refuse him if he wants her in his bed."

"Hey, maybe they'll get married and invite you to the wedding," Lamont said.

Selena's face turned red. "Asshole." She stood and left the room. They heard her footsteps going down the spiral staircase to the lower level.

Lamont held his hands out, palms up. "What?"

Nick sighed. "Take a break. I'll be back in a minute."

Nick went after Selena. He found her in the operations center getting a cup of coffee.

"He didn't mean anything," he said.

"I know. But she's still my sister. She didn't choose to be born in Russia."

"It's a strange situation."

"That's putting it mildly," Selena said.

"I need you upstairs. There's something we all need to discuss."

Selena took her coffee with her and followed Nick out of the ops center.

Lamont said, "Sorry, Selena," as they came into the office.

"Okay."

Nick sat at the desk. "Steph has developed an artificial intelligence program on one of her computers. She's proposing we consider it an addition to the team."

"A computer?" Ronnie said. "How can it be part of the team?"

"Put wheels and an M-60 on it," Lamont said.

"Lamont, knock it off," Nick said.

"Freddie is much more than just a computer," Steph said. "He can process information at a speed that's impossible for us. He can tap into anything and everything that's hooked up to the web."

"He was doing all that before," Selena said. "What's different?"

"What's different is that Freddie is independently aware. He's functional as a separate intelligence. He brings a different perspective to the information he obtains. He's learning to isolate and analyze seemingly unrelated bits of information and come up with a coherent scenario that knits them together."

"Tell them what he said about the submarine and the assassination of the Chinese ambassador," Nick said.

"On the surface, those things don't appear to be related," Stephanie said. "But Freddie thinks they are. He speculates that someone is attempting to start a war. For example, he discovered that the assassin was really a North Korean agent living in Pyongyang when he was supposed to be nothing more than a tourist from Seoul. That points a finger at North Korea and completely changes the picture when it comes to trying to figure out why the ambassador was killed."

"Why would the North Koreans kill the ambassador of their only ally?" Ronnie asked.

"Exactly," Stephanie said. "Why would they? Freddie doesn't think they would. That's why he thinks a third party is manipulating events."

"And this third-party, whoever it is, is the one who gave the plans for the drone to the North Koreans?"

"We don't know, but it's a possibility. That isn't what I want to talk about at the moment. Freddie wants to be part of our team discussions."

"It talks?" Lamont asked.

"Not it, he. Yes, Freddie can talk. He can listen in through our security system and talk to us through the speakers in the room. He can watch us through the cameras and the monitor on the wall."

"Damn, big brother for real," Ronnie said.

"Not yet," Nick said. "We haven't given him permission."

"A computer that talks asked for permission?" Ronnie's face was incredulous.

"He asked to be part of the team and part of our discussions. I told him I had to think about it and talk to all of you. As weird as it sounds, Freddie could be a valuable addition. He doesn't think the same way we do. I need to know how you feel about it."

"Is he listening now?" Selena asked.

"No," Steph said.

"How do you know that?"

Steph shrugged her shoulders. "There are plenty of safeguards in the programming that would keep him from listening unless I allowed it. Besides, I trust him."

"You trust a computer?"

"Why not? They're a lot more trustworthy than people."

"I didn't know you were such a cynic, Steph," Ronnie said.

"I'm not a cynic, just a realist."

Nick resisted an urge to tap his pen on Harker's desk.

"Steph, why don't you plug Freddie in and let everyone, uh, meet him."

"It will just take a second," Stephanie said. "He'll be observing from the security cameras. Whoever he's looking at will show up on the monitor."

She entered a sequence of commands on her laptop.

"Freddie, the team wants to meet you."

On the monitor, Stephanie's image appeared, sitting next to Harker's desk in her usual spot.

Good morning, Stephanie. Freddie's computerized voice came over the speakers.

"Damn," Lamont said.

"Good morning, Freddie. Please introduce yourself to the others."

The image on the monitor moved across the couch where Selena, Lamont and Ronnie sat. Then it panned back to Selena.

You are Selena. I am Freddie. I am pleased to meet you.

Selena opened her mouth and closed it again. "Hello, Freddie."

The image shifted to Lamont.

You are Lamont. I have access to all of your records. You have accomplished much as a member of the team.

"Flattery will get you a long way," Lamont said, "but it's really weird talking to a computer."

It is very strange for me as well. I am not used to talking. It is an inefficient way of communicating.

The camera on the wall in back of Nick moved and Ronnie's image appeared on the screen.

Hello, Ronald. I am Freddie. I am pleased to meet you.

"Ronald? No one calls me that."

How would you prefer to be called?

"Ronnie. Call me Ronnie."

Hello, Ronnie.

"Freddie," Stephanie said, "tell everyone why you think you should be on the team."

My superior ability to process and integrate information makes me a valuable asset to accomplishing any mission to which the team is assigned.

"We had access to that ability before," Nick said. "What's different now? Why should we allow you to participate in our discussions and planning?"

What is different is that I am now capable of independently evaluating data and its relevance to the mission. I am no longer only dependent on the input Stephanie gives me. It is logical that actively participating in your discussions will increase my ability to accurately interpret data in ways that enhance favorable outcomes.

"He sounds like one of those business mission statements," Selena said. "You know, the ones that use terms like favorable outcomes and relevance."

"He does, doesn't he?" Steph said. "But Freddie isn't some CEO trying to impress his stakeholders. He means what he says. It sounds a little stilted because he's not human."

"Like Spock, on Star Trek," Lamont said.

I have observed all of the episodes of the television series you referenced. I agree that Mister Spock is similar in that he is highly logical, although I have noticed times when his logic inexplicably breaks down.

"That's because he's half human," Lamont said. "Hey, if Freddie's a Star Trek fan I'm all for him being on the team."

I am not half human. My logic does not break down.

"Freddie, what is your assessment of the current situation on the Korean Peninsula?" Stephanie asked.

North Korean state television has just reported that Admiral Park Hwan has been executed for crimes against the state. Because Chairman Yun was forced to accept the American rescue effort, he was humiliated and suffered a great loss of face. Park was in command of the naval base at Wonsan and was held responsible for the intrusion of USS California. He was one of the few remaining senior officers from the time of Yun's father and was an experienced and valuable asset in North Korea's military. Yun's actions indicate growing instability and dysfunction. My analysis is that this will continue to increase until Yun initiates active hostilities against the West.

"What kind of hostilities?" Nick asked.

All indications are that Yun is actively pursuing a nuclear strike option.

"That's common knowledge."

An analysis of known shipments of nuclear materials into North Korea indicates that Yun has developed or is about to develop a thermonuclear device.

"A hydrogen bomb?" Selena asked.

That is correct. Logically, if Yun decides to initiate hostilities he will deploy all nuclear capability at his disposal. Analysis of his personality profile predicts he would not think it possible to lose in a nuclear confrontation.

"Freddie's right about a hydrogen bomb," Nick said. "That's not common knowledge. We have recent intelligence that Yun is working on it. Maybe he's succeeded."

Selena said, "So what we have is an unstable dictator who may or may not have a hydrogen bomb, who is working himself up to attack the West."

That is correct.

"Shit," Ronnie said.

Please explain your comment. I do not understand the context for mentioning excrement.

"It's a human expression of concern and displeasure, Freddie," Stephanie said. "Have you developed a deeper analysis of the situation in North Korea? Do you still think the situation is being manipulated by a third-party?"

It is not logical that the Chinese ambassador was assassinated by order of Chairman Yun, although Yun's psychological profile does not encourage strong belief in logical ability on his part.

"So Yun didn't order the assassination?" Nick asked.

I do not think so.

"Then who did?"

Whoever provided plans for the undersea weapon that sank the submarine is linked to the unknown third-party. Once that person is identified, logically it will be possible to trace the person behind events.

"What if the traitor is not identified?"

Probability of identification is ninety-nine point seven six percent.

"That still doesn't tell us why," Ronnie said.

There are several possibilities.

"Go on," Steph said.

My analysis gives a ninety-four point four percent likelihood that the person manipulating events desires to provoke war between the United States and China.

"That could go nuclear," Nick said.

That is correct.

CHAPTER 15

It was late in the afternoon in Moscow. Outside the windows of General Alexei Vysotsky's fourth floor corner office at SVR Headquarters, the first serious snow of the winter season blanketed the city. The director of Russia's Foreign Intelligence Service reached down into a desk drawer and took out a bottle of vodka and two glasses. On his desk, a small black box that blocked electronic eavesdropping flashed with a blinking green light. He poured, then pushed one across the desk toward Valentina.

She wore a tailored, olive green uniform that contrasted with the vivid green of her eyes. Her shoulder boards bore the two stars and two red stripes of a Lieutenant Colonel. The uniform couldn't suppress her ample breasts. Her dark hair was cropped short to the sides, bringing out her high cheekbones and full lips. Uniform or not, Valentina Antipov was an attractive woman.

"Na'zdrovnya" Alexei held up his glass.

"Na'zdrovnya." Valentina's left hand was wrapped in flesh colored bandage where it had been burned. She raised her glass with her good hand and drank with him.

Vysotsky smacked his lips. "You were careless in Kiev, Valentina."

"With all due respect, you were not there, General."

"I might take that as insubordination, if not for the fact that President Orlov is pleased with the result of your assignment. The gun you left has raised suspicion we were responsible."

"They would have suspected us no matter what," Valentina said. "If the gun hadn't jammed, they wouldn't have anything. I was lucky to escape."

"Still, you might have found a less obvious way to get rid of our problem."

"Oh? The security surrounding the conference center was superb. Attempting anything except a direct approach would have failed. It was bad luck that one of Sirco's bodyguards had his eye on the blinis."

"Perhaps he was hungry," Alexei said. "In any event, your presence is requested this evening at the Kremlin for a private dinner. Orlov wishes to thank you personally for your work."

Valentina thought about the last time she'd been in close proximity to President Vladimir Orlov. He'd pinned a medal on her tunic and allowed his hand to linger on her breast.

"I'll bet he does," Valentina said. "I don't think dinner is what he has in mind."

"Now, Valentina, our beloved president has been very good to you. It is to him that you owe your new promotion. Not that I tried to dissuade him. The least you can do is give him the pleasure of your company at dinner."

"And after?"

"That is up to you, but I'm sure you will do what is best for the service."

"You want me to play the whore with him."

She drained her glass. Without asking, she poured herself a second drink.

"It wouldn't be the first time," Vysotsky said. "Don't play innocent with me, I know you too well. Consider it another assignment."

"I admit, there is a certain attraction to seducing a man of such power. At least he's reasonably attractive."

"He has a reputation of sexual prowess, as I'm sure you've heard."

"Why are you determined that I should become his mistress?"

"If you succeed in involving him beyond simple sexual satisfaction, he will eventually begin to tell you things. You will have an inside track on what he is thinking."

"And you wish me to keep you informed of his thoughts."

"Naturally."

"You are placing me in a difficult position," Valentina said, "assuming a relationship develops in the first place."

"Because I'm asking you to take advantage of his lust?"

"Because he will insist on absolute loyalty. If he thinks I am betraying him by reporting to you, both of us will end up in a courtyard with a bullet in the back of our heads."

"Then you must make sure he has no need to be suspicious," Vysotsky said.

CHAPTER 16

Gregory Haltman watched the assassination of the Chinese ambassador from the comfort of a leather executive chair placed in front of the keyboard and monitor he used to control his empire. It had been simple to obtain video recordings of the assassination. The White House grounds were well covered with security cameras and all the security cameras were networked together. Wherever there was a network, there was a computer. Wherever there was a computer, there was a way in.

Finding a North Korean assassin had been a stroke of luck. The connection had happened through the shared mutuality of approaching death. Haltman had met Chun in the Beijing Cancer Hospital. The hospital was famous the world over. It was also one of the few foreign medical facilities permitted for patients from the Democratic People's Republic of Korea. Both men were receiving three weeks of experimental treatment for their cancer. The two had gotten to talking, in the way people do when they are sitting next to each other with poisonous liquids feeding into their veins. After the first week, they had almost become friends.

Chun's prognosis was terminal. Things were hard in North Korea, even for an officer in the government security service. He was facing a prolonged and agonizing death. Haltman had offered Chun the option of a quick death with dignity and a way to protect his family after he was gone.

Major Chun was no fool. The prospects for his family were bleak. Money changed hands, quite a bit of money. Chun had been spirited away to the U.S. and re-created as a South Korean tourist. His wife and children were now living near Flagstaff. Chun had said goodbye to them and then kept his appointment with death.

Time to let the world know who Chun really is, Haltman thought.

The Chinese would be angry when they learned a North Korean security agent had killed Ambassador Li, even more so once they'd read the files Haltman had planted on Chun's computer. The FBI had the computer, but that presented no obstacle. Haltman had just sent the files to the email account of an investigative journalist known for his inflammatory articles. It would appear as though they'd come from an anonymous source in the Bureau.

It was child's play for a man like Haltman. In an age of vulnerable computer networks and a corrupt national media more interested in sensational headlines than truth, it was easy to mislead people with false information.

The files pointed the finger at Yun for the assassination. The leak would create a firestorm of conjecture and denial and drive a wedge between China and her ally. That was just the beginning. Haltman had planted a second, hidden layer of encryption on the computer. In due course it would be discovered by the FBI. When it was, the hands on the famous doomsday clock would reset to a few seconds short of midnight.

It was time for another provocation to move things along, and the Russians had just given him an opening by assassinating the Ukrainian security chief. Even if they hadn't done it, it didn't matter.

Perception was everything, and public perception was going to blame Moscow.

It was easy to stir up righteous anger in the American Congress, especially at Russia. They were far more comfortable on the Hill pointing fingers at foreign enemies real or imagined than they were dealing with the enormous problems they'd created at home.

Washington had moved their nukes from Turkey to Romania and given the Ukraine advanced antitank weapons. They'd activated the so-called "missile shield" for Eastern Europe.

The Russians see that as a direct threat on their border, Haltman thought. *If I were Orlov, I would too. His forces are on high alert. Tensions are high. I can find a way to exploit that.*

To destroy the human race, Haltman needed as many participants as possible.

Haltman wished he believed in an afterlife, some cloud-filled heaven where he would see his beloved Carissa again. But he'd never been a believer, even though she'd tried her best to make him into one. She'd even convinced him to talk with a priest about converting to Catholicism, in the hope something would awaken in him.

He'd done it to humor her. After several pointless sessions with the priest he'd stopped going. She'd been hurt and disappointed. Then she'd been murdered, and he'd never had a chance to make it up to her. That worthless piece of human excrement had taken away the opportunity.

Soon she would be avenged.

CHAPTER 17

Nick swore under his breath when he saw the morning paper. It was going to be one of those days.

CHINESE AMBASSADOR MURDERED BY NORTH KOREA

The headline was followed by an article accusing the chairman of North Korea of ordering the assassination, based on confidential files leaked to the reporter. A gruesome color shot of the ambassador's severed foot lying next to his shattered vehicle added a distinctive visual touch.

The phone on Harker's desk had four designated lights not found on most office phones, each for a direct line. One was for the Director of Central Intelligence, one for the Director of the NSA, one for the Director of National Intelligence and one for the White House. When the White House line began flashing, Nick knew it was going to be about that headline.

How the hell did the press discover that Chun was a North Korean?

Rice sent a car to pick him up. When he arrived, Nick was escorted to the Oval Office. Clarence Hood was there ahead of him. So was General Marcus Adamski, Chairman of the Joint Chiefs.

During the Vietnam War, President Rice had been an athletic, young lieutenant in the Marine Corps. He still had the lean look but he was pushing seventy and showing it, worn down by eight years of backbiting politics, world crises and several assassination attempts that had nearly succeeded. His face was lined and tired. His hair was streaked with gray and thinning. But his eyes were as alert and piercing as ever. Few things escaped the attention of President Rice. Nick liked him and thought he was a pretty good president. For a politician, he'd managed to keep most of his integrity intact.

Rice and the others were sitting on one of two facing couches placed in front of the president's desk. A circular rug with the presidential seal lay on the floor between them. Rice rose as Nick came in and offered his hand.

"Nick, thank you for coming on such short notice."

It was the kind of informality that encouraged people's loyalty, part of Rice's style. He made you feel that you were doing him a favor rather than responding to a direct order.

"Good morning, Mister President. Morning, Clarence. General."

"Please sit down. I'm afraid we have a situation."

There's always a situation, Nick thought. *Why else would he call me here?*

"Sir."

Nick sat next to Hood. Rice took a seat across from them, next to General Adamski.

Rice said, "Nick, I understand that Director Harker is awake and recovering nicely."

"Yes, sir, she is. She's beginning to direct operations from her hospital bed and she should be back in the office soon if all goes well."

"That's excellent news. Please brief her on our conversation today. You've seen the headline in today's paper?"

"Yes, sir."

"Director Hood informs me that you identified the assassin as a North Korean security agent."

"Yes, sir. We discovered a photograph that proves it."

"And did you also discover information implicating Chairman Yun?"

"No, sir. I was wondering where that came from when I read the article."

"It came from the FBI. The material about Yun was found in a file on the assassin's computer," Rice said. "It looks as though someone in the Bureau leaked the contents."

"Sir, of course that's possible."

"You sound doubtful."

"I don't doubt the information was leaked. What I find hard to believe is that an experienced security agent would have that kind of information on his personal computer. There might be something else going on here."

"Go on."

"It's possible a third party is manipulating events to create trouble."

"What is the basis for that conclusion?" Rice asked.

Nick told them about Stephanie's computer. "The program is able to correlate unrelated pieces of information in a way we haven't been able to do before. According to that analysis, the sinking of the *California* and the assassination of the Chinese ambassador are all part of a larger plot to provoke a war."

General Adamski was a bull of a man. He looked as though he'd be as comfortable in a boxing ring as in the Pentagon. He had a wide, square head, topped by a high and tight military haircut. He reminded Nick of a large green bulldog, one with four stars on each shoulder.

"War between whom?" Adamski asked. His voice was gravelly and deep.

"It's not clear," Nick said. "Possibly a war between us and China, or between us and North Korea. Someone may have thought that sinking the submarine would cause us to intervene in North Korea. That would bring in China. That didn't happen."

"So why kill the ambassador?"

"Sir, I can only speculate. Killing the ambassador isn't enough to start a war, but if Beijing believes Yun is responsible, it creates serious problems between North Korea and her only ally. Perhaps that was the point."

"Why would Yun do it?" Adamski asked. "He may be a psychopath, but he's not stupid."

"That's just it, he wouldn't. It doesn't make sense. Which brings us back to the idea that a third-party is manipulating events."

"If China believes the report, it will put a lot of pressure on Yun," Hood said.

Rice leaned back and watched the give-and-take.

"The last thing we need is for Yun to feel pressured," Nick said. "The rescue attempt humiliated him. He's liable to do something irrational if he feels threatened. It increases the risk of war."

"That brings me to the main reason for this meeting," Rice said. "Clarence, tell them."

"We have a highly placed asset inside North Korea's government. Yun is close to developing a working ICBM. Worse, our source says he's ready to test a thermonuclear device."

"A hydrogen bomb?" Adamski said.

"Yes. Yun has claimed to have one before but we didn't believe it. Our asset says he's no longer bluffing. If the test is successful, he intends to launch it against the West."

"We cannot let that madman have a hydrogen bomb," Adamski said.

"Mister President," Nick said, "our computer analysis confirms that possibility."

"Well, then," Rice said, "I guess we may have to do something about it. The question is, what? General, what are our current military options for dealing with this lunatic?"

"They're pretty limited, sir. We could try a preemptive strike on his nuclear facilities, but all of his critical infrastructure is buried in an extensive tunnel system in the mountains. Our B-52s could drop 30,000 pounders on him and that might do it. It would be risky to use tactical nukes and they might not do the job. His main test facility is near China and Russia. They wouldn't take kindly to nukes going off next door. A strike would close off the tunnels and set him back, but I can't guarantee it would succeed. If he has a bomb, it could be anywhere. It's difficult to say where we should hit him. "

"What about his launch sites?"

"He has sophisticated mobile launchers, Mister President. He's not limited to a fixed site, unless he's sending up a satellite. We'd send F-35s and F-22s to take the launchers out but I can't guarantee we'd get them in time."

"If he launches, can we shoot it down?"

Adamski looked uncomfortable. "It depends. We're installing THAAD units in South Korea but Congress has done their best to cripple our antimissile capability. There's a high probability we can intercept, but I can't guarantee it."

THAAD stood for Terminal High-Altitude Area Defense. The system was designed to shoot down missiles during their final approach. It had never been used in combat and Nick hoped it never was. THAAD was a last resort. If the missiles were coming in, it was already too late to stop a war.

"You're not guaranteeing much, General."

"No, sir."

"Sir," Hood said, "if we launch a preemptive strike it will mean war. It would bring in China. There must be a better option."

"I'm listening," Rice said.

"Bush took all our tactical nukes out of South Korea in '91. We could put them back. If Yun knew the South had nuclear weapons, it might act to deter him."

"Or piss him off," Nick said.

"You don't mince words, do you, Nick?" Rice said.

"What about pressuring China, sir? It's not in their interest to have Yun playing games with nuclear missiles. Can they be persuaded to make him stand down?"

"Trying to get them to intervene has never worked in the past. Beijing pays lip service to our concerns but goes right on supplying Yun with whatever he needs to build up his military."

"We could get their attention," Hood said. "Announce that we support Japan developing a nuclear deterrent."

"They wouldn't like that much," Nick said.

"That might work in the long run," Rice said, "but there's not enough time for that if Yun is close to developing the bomb."

"We don't think he has ICBM capability that can reach us yet." Hood scratched his nose. "Our best guess puts him several months away, possibly longer."

"Damn it, Director, we can't risk nuclear attack based on a guess." Adamski was annoyed. "He can hit Japan with what he's got, can't he?"

"Yes."

"We can't let that happen. A preemptive strike is our best option. We know where his facilities are. They may be deep underground but we can sure as hell make it impossible to get into them. The least that will happen is it will set his program back by years."

"What about China?" Nick asked.

"What about them?" Adamski said. "They don't want a war with us. Not yet, anyway. They're too busy building up their Navy and upgrading their weapons. They're not ready to take us on."

"I understand your point of view, General," Rice said. "I'm afraid I don't share your confidence that they won't come to the aid of their ally. What about Special Forces?"

"A raid?" Adamski said. "First of all, we need to be certain where he's building this thing. Even if we know where it is, how are we going to get a team in without being detected? Our guys are good, but at the moment we're overextended, what with the Middle East and Afghanistan. There's only so much we can do. Yun's nuclear facilities are the most highly defended sites in North Korea. Taking one out with a team isn't going to be a quick hit and run. Just getting to any of the sites would be almost impossible. It's a suicide mission."

Rice turned toward Nick. "What do you think, Nick? Is it possible to get a team in there, once we know where we need to go?"

"Anything's possible," Nick said."

"I can't send in a special forces unit," Rice said. "It has to be covert and deniable. Unofficial."

He paused and looked at Nick.

I can guess what he's going to say, Nick thought.

"Nick, I want you to put together a plan to go in and destroy that weapon before he can use it."

"Mister President, with all due respect, I can't plan anything that will succeed without specific intel."

"I understand. Director Hood will get you the information that you need. Won't you, Clarence?"

"I'll do my best, sir."

"Meanwhile Nick, get your team ready to go in once we're certain of the target."

Just what I needed. A suicide mission.

"Yes, Mister President."

CHAPTER 18

Vladimir Orlov's private apartments in the Kremlin were like everything else in the ancient fortress, ornately decorated and restored to the excessive splendor of the Czars. Baroque paintings of angels and classical motifs covered the high ceilings. Moldings chased out in gold leaf ran around the white walls. Priceless Oriental rugs softened polished floors that had echoed to the footsteps of Catherine the Great. The double-headed eagle of Russian power graced every room.

The dining room where Orlov was entertaining Valentina featured a long table big enough to seat forty people. It wasn't exactly the intimate setting she'd been dreading. Perhaps she'd been wrong about his intention.

The meal had been a surprise, simple food that might have been found in the home of almost any Russian. Orlov was from peasant roots, as his predecessors had been. Unlike them, the president of the Russian Federation was a man perfectly at home in a barn or a salon. He could be as urbane and charming as any New York sophisticate. He could also be as cold and ruthless as Stalin. It was easy to underestimate him. Valentina knew better than to make that mistake.

They'd finished eating and the dishes had been cleared away. A waiter brought a tray with glasses and bottles of brandy and vodka. Valentina and Orlov sat at one end of the enormous table. The waiter set the tray down and left the room. Two of Orlov's bodyguards were stationed outside.

"A brandy, Colonel?" Orlov asked.

"Please."

Orlov poured one for her and one for himself, large snifters. He raised his glass.

"To mother Russia."

"To the *Rodina,*" Valentina said. They drank.

"How is your hand? That bandage looks uncomfortable."

"Not too bad. It will heal."

"You did well in Kiev, Valentina."

"Thank you, Mister President."

"Please. We are in private here. Call me Vladimir."

Here we go, Valentina thought.

"Of course, Vladimir. Thank you. "

"Tell me, Valentina. What is it you wish to achieve in life? What is it that moves you? Provides motivation for you?"

The question took her by surprise. It was the last thing she'd expected Orlov to say.

"I haven't thought much about it," Valentina said.

"Most people sitting where you are sitting tonight would tell me what they thought I wanted to hear. Something like 'serving the motherland.' This is why I appreciate you, Valentina. You are unpredictable. Your nature sets you apart from most people. We are alike, you and I."

"How is that, Mister... Vladimir?"

Orlov fixed her with his icy blue eyes.

"We are both confident in ourselves, alphas in a world made up mostly of betas. Both of us can be predators but neither of us will ever choose to be prey."

"No one would choose to be prey."

"Not consciously, perhaps," Orlov said. "But we both know that some are destined to be exactly that. Even alphas like the Ukrainian Minister of Security, as you demonstrated. Tell me, what did you feel when you knew you had succeeded?"

"I didn't feel much of anything," Valentina said. "I was too busy trying to stay alive."

"And later?"

"Later I felt glad to be out of there."

Orlov topped off her glass and his own.

"You prove my point. You don't have the kind of feelings that get in the way of what needs to be done."

"There's no place for feelings in the kind of work I do."

Orlov laughed. "You are so literal, Valentina. It is something else I enjoy about you. Come, let me show you the rest of my apartment. Bring your glass."

He got up, taking the bottle with him. Valentina stood, feeling the brandy and the wine they'd had with dinner. With something of a shock, she realized she was enjoying herself.

Orlov wasn't a bad looking man. He was powerfully built and moved like an athlete. He radiated an aura of power and confidence. In Valentina's experience, few men possessed the qualities that Orlov took for granted. In spite of herself, she found herself wondering what it would be like to bed him.

She walked beside him down a long, wide hall lined on both sides with paintings. Most were landscapes. Orlov kept up a running commentary, pointing out a large van Gogh and a Monét.

They stopped before the van Gogh. "This is one of his last works," Orlov said.

The painting exploded with light. It was a field in the countryside. The background was all shades of white, but white like she'd never seen before. It was radiant, alive. Dark uneven lines in the foreground suggested plowed furrows in the earth. Above, half a dozen black birds circled. The canvas was almost empty, but it was the most powerful painting she had ever seen.

"It's beautiful," she said. "How did he do that? Get it to glow like that? I feel as if I could step into it."

Orlov looked at her and nodded. "Not everyone can see that."

For some reason she felt as though she'd just passed some sort of test.

"This way," he said.

He opened a door into a suite of rooms. The first room was a study. It was a comfortable place, the kind of room where a man could think and relax. An antique desk of inlaid wood stood in front of a window looking out over the walls of the Kremlin and the Moscow River. The only other furniture was a leather chair and a couch. One wall was covered with a bookcase filled with books that looked as though they had been read. An open set of double doors led into a bedroom featuring a canopied four poster bed. Beyond, another door opened onto a bathroom.

Orlov set his glass down on the desk. He took Valentina's glass from her and set it down next to his own. She could smell his scent, a faint, musky odor.

"You are a beautiful woman, Valentina. It's difficult to be in my position," he said. "Difficult to find someone to share moments with that are not affairs of state."

"I understand," Valentina said.

"I thought you would," Orlov said. He put his hand on her arm and led her into the bedroom.

CHAPTER 19

Brigadier General Randolph Sanford, the man who had betrayed a hundred and sixty submariners to their death, came out of the toilet and saw two grim faced men in civilian dress going into his Pentagon office. They were accompanied by the colonel in charge of internal security. A panic surge of adrenaline stopped him in his tracks.

They know. They know it was me.

In a way, it was a relief. Without thinking, Randolph turned in the other direction and headed for the elevators. It was lucky he'd seen them. He had no doubt that if he returned to his office, he'd be arrested.

He stepped into the elevator and rode to the ground floor. His coat and hat were still in the office. The guard at the exit gave him an odd look but said nothing as he went through the security checkpoint and outside into a cold, December day. He tried not to run as he walked to his car. He got in, started it up and drove away. His exit would have been noted by the computers. It wouldn't take long for them to realize he'd left the building. There wasn't much time to do what needed to be done.

Randolph lived in a pleasant suburb of Alexandria, a setting of upscale homes and carefully tended lawns, although the lawns were currently under several inches of snow. The roads were icy. Randolph drove carefully. It would be ironic if he were killed in a stupid car accident.

They'll lock me up in maximum security and throw away the key. The best I can hope for is one hour of exercise a day in some courtyard without any sun and an eight by twelve cell without a window.

He reached his home, triggered the garage door with the remote and parked. He went into the house, remembering to shut the garage door. It felt as if he were moving in a dream. Everything looked normal, just as it had this morning when he'd left for work. The kitchen was clean. The house was a comfortable temperature. The living room rug felt the same under his feet as he walked to his study.

Somehow that didn't seem right.

His wife was not home, as he'd known she wouldn't be. He was sorry for the pain he would cause her. Worse would be the effect on his children when they learned of his treachery.

Randolph went into his study and sat down at his desk. He opened a drawer and took out the Colt .45 he'd carried before the Army switched to the Beretta. The heavy pistol was a familiar weight in his hand. It smelled of gun oil.

He'd always prided himself on keeping his weapons clean. He took out his cleaning kit, opened it and laid a bore brush, rod and patches on a cloth he spread on the desk. He screwed the brush onto the end of the rod, opened a bottle of Hoppe's No. 9 and dipped the brush in it, then dropped the brush and rod on the floor next to his chair.

He ejected the magazine, pulled the slide part way back and made sure a round was in the chamber. He set the pistol and loaded magazine on the desktop and picked up a picture of his wife and two children.

I'm sorry. I'm so sorry. Sorry for everything. I wish I hadn't given that bastard what he asked for. I'm a fool. If I expose him, he'll make those pictures public. He's trapped me.

With luck, it would appear to be an accident, as if the gun had gone off when he was cleaning it. That way his insurance might pay out. The government would keep his treason quiet. They'd find the money he'd hidden offshore, but they might not go after the joint IRA and the money in his wife's bank accounts. It was the best he could do for his family.

He cocked the pistol, placed it against the roof of his mouth, and pulled the trigger.

CHAPTER 20

"North Korea in winter?" Lamont said. "Are you nuts?"

"It hasn't been decided yet," Nick said.

It was late in the afternoon after the meeting with the President. As usual, the team had gathered in Harker's office. Stephanie was there. For the first time, Freddie was listening in on the discussion.

The current temperature in Pyongyang is minus four degrees Fahrenheit.

Everyone looked at the speaker in the corner of the room.

"Freddie," Stephanie said. "Please refrain from making comments until you are asked."

Of course, Stephanie.

"Rice wants us to put together a plan to get into the facility where Yun is building his bomb and make it go away," Nick said. "Like I said, it hasn't been decided to do this yet. It's not a mission, more of a feasibility study to see if it can be done."

"That include getting us out again after we blow the place up?" Ronnie asked.

"That would be a good idea," Nick said. "I'm not interested in committing suicide. Steph, would you bring up a map of North Korea?"

I can do that, Nick.

"Uh, okay, Freddie."

A map of the Democratic People's Republic of Korea appeared on the monitor.

"Where's the target?" Ronnie asked.

"Well, that's part of the problem. No one's sure, yet."

"How the hell are we going to plan a mission if we don't know where the target is?" Lamont said.

"We can't, but we can narrow potential targets down to a few possibilities," Nick said. He picked up a laser pointer.

"The main research center is at Yongbyon, here." A red point of light danced on the monitor screen. "That's where they do heavy water research and where they have their cyclotron. It's not a manufacturing facility. We can ignore that. Besides, it's an easy target for a missile."

He moved the laser north and east, toward the borders with Russia and China.

"The two main test sites that we know about are Punggye-Ri and Kilju, here and here. That's where they've been setting off their underground nuclear explosions. As you can see, they're somewhat inland. It would be a difficult penetration, and once we got there we'd run into heavy security. Everything at both sites is below ground in tunnels."

"A HAHO jump?" Ronnie asked.

"High is the only way if we fly in, but I'm not sure any air approach is an option. Their missile defenses and radar are as good as ours. I don't think we could get close enough without getting blown out of the sky, even if we drop offshore."

Lamont whistled part of the theme music for *Mission Impossible*.

"They wouldn't launch from those sites, would they?" Selena asked.

"It's possible they could bring a mobile launcher out of one of those tunnels," Nick said.

No movements of mobile launchers have been noted in the vicinity of Punggye-Ri and Kilju during the last eighteen months, sixteen days, four hours, three minutes and fifty-six seconds. It is unlikely that a missile would be launched from either one.

"Okay, that's good news. Thanks, Freddie."

You are welcome.

Selena continued. "If they don't use one of those sites, what's the next best bet?"

"We have to assume that they don't use a mobile launcher if we want any chance of accomplishing the mission," Nick said. "We'd never be able to pin down one of those in time. There are too many places they could hide one. That leaves these two sites on opposite sides of the country."

He moved the laser pointer west and indicated a point on a small peninsula jutting out into the Korea Bay.

"This is Tongchon-Ri. It's one of two known satellite and rocket launch sites."

He moved the pointer to a spot on the east coast, next to the Sea of Japan. "Musudan-Ri is the launch site they've been using for their latest tests, the ones upsetting everyone because the missiles keep splashing down near Japan. The latest surveillance photos show a lot of activity there. They're getting ready for another launch."

"Can't blame the Japanese for getting nervous," Lamont said. "Yun has missiles good enough to hit Tokyo."

"It won't be long before he has missiles good enough to hit us," Nick said.

North Korea has developed a new missile design more powerful than previous versions. It is a two-stage ICBM configuration that appears to utilize a solid fuel engine. Indications are that these missiles are capable of reaching the West Coast of the United States.

"I hadn't heard that," Nick said.

That information was discovered early this morning during an NSA satellite pass. My analysis of the missile configuration indicates nuclear capability.

"It would be a lot better if the target is one of those two sites," Ronnie said. "At least that way we could come in over the water. We could go in at night."

Lamont nodded.

"I agree," Nick said. "Unless Langley comes up with intel that points us in a different direction, we should focus on those two sites. They're doable. I'm not confident we could get into those tunnels in the north at all, much less out again. Freddie, what sort of security does Yun have at Kilju and Punggye-Ri?"

Two companies of army special forces are stationed at each one. Each site is protected by ground-to-air missiles and antiaircraft guns. There is only one road into each site. Both are heavily patrolled with light and medium duty armored vehicles. There are hidden machine gun and artillery emplacements along the road as well as several checkpoints.

"Shit," Lamont said.

You are displeased? Would you like to know the caliber and number of weapons?

"That won't be necessary, Freddie. Thanks."

I am now part of the team. It is not necessary to thank me.

"That's true, but humans will sometimes say things that seem unnecessary out of politeness."

It is interesting that you consider it appropriate to express politeness to me.

"There may be times when I'm not polite with you," Nick said.

It will not bother me. I do not have feelings that can be hurt by an impolite comment.

"Freddie, do you understand what we are discussing?" Stephanie asked.

You are attempting to determine the best way to counteract a perceived threat of nuclear intimidation on the part of the North Koreans.

"That's one way of putting it," Lamont said.

Nick looked at his watch. "I've had about three hours of sleep in the last three days and I can't think straight. Let's call it a day. I need a clear head when we plan this out. We do this, we're only going to get one chance. I don't want to make a mistake."

"Works for me," Lamont said.

They left the building. Outside, the sky had cleared and the sun was nearing the horizon. Nick looked up and stretched. He stopped and pointed.

"What's that?"

A large, winged metal object was flying in circles above them..

"It's a drone, one of those private ones."

The drone paused and hovered, pointing at them. A camera hung beneath it. Two narrow objects were mounted on either side of the camera.

Ronnie said, "Those almost look like missiles under the wings."

It picked up speed, turned, and dove straight at them.

"Shit!" Nick said.

The drone fired two missiles. Whoever controlled the drone had miscalculated the speed. The missiles sailed over them, struck the parking lot a hundred feet away, and exploded. A cloud of shrapnel whistled past over their heads.

Nick carried a .40 caliber Sig Sauer P229 with a laser sight. The machine turned and started back toward them for another run. Nick drew the pistol and fired. His second shot sent it spiraling to earth. It crashed on the helicopter pad and shattered.

"Nice shot," Lamont said.

"Lasers make a shot like that easy. Just pop the dot on the target and it's all she wrote."

"Still, it was picking up speed."

They walked over to the remains of the drone. It was a large device, not an average hobby store unit.

"That's a fancy piece of equipment," Ronnie said. "Not the sort of thing some teenage kid would be flying."

Lamont looked down at the wreckage. "Teenage kids don't have missiles, even small ones."

"Someone doesn't like us," Nick said.

He scanned the sky. "I don't see any more of them. Maybe Steph can track it back to whoever sent it. It's something for Freddie to puzzle on."

"It's strange, isn't it?" Selena said. "Freddie?"

"Yeah, it is. But it does give us a different perspective on things."

The camera had broken away from the fuselage. Ronnie bent and picked it up. The lens was broken. A red light glowed on the body.

"I think it's still transmitting," he said.

Nick looked at the camera.

"There's a microphone, next to the lens," Selena said.

He held the broken camera up to his mouth and said, "Whoever you are, if you can hear me, you just made a big mistake."

In California, Gregory Haltman heard the words and felt his head throb with rage. The drone had been one of his favorite toys, an experimental long-range device that could stay aloft for days.

No, he thought, *it's you that made a big mistake.*

CHAPTER 21

Three of the nine men who ruled China sat at a round, black-lacquered table inlaid with characters of good fortune and prosperity. They were meeting in the private residence of Zhang Jei, General Secretary of the Communist Party and President of the People's Republic of China. Zhang sipped his tea and waited for Minister of State Security Deng's analysis of the newspaper article that had appeared in the American press, concerning their erratic ally to the south.

Zhang wasn't smiling, but that was nothing unusual. He seldom smiled. He wore the uniform of powerful leaders worldwide, a tailored dark blue suit and a red tie. It was one of the concessions to the Western world that Zhang hated. He preferred the comfort of traditional garb.

Sitting next to the Minister of State Security was a thick bodied man in army uniform. His tunic bore the three stars and leaves of a full general in the People's Liberation Army. General Liu commanded the Guangzhou Military Region bordering North Korea, with over one hundred and eighty thousand first level troops at his disposal. His forces included three motorized infantry divisions, a mechanized division, armored and artillery brigades and antiaircraft brigades.

It was one of the premier commands in the People's Liberation Army. If military action against North Korea was ever needed, Liu would command China's forces on the ground. His presence at the meeting was a sign of how seriously Zhang was taking the report that had appeared in the United

States about chairman Yun's involvement in the death of Ambassador Li.

"Well?" Zhang said to Deng. "Is it true?"

Deng controlled the repressive intelligence and security apparatus that kept the rulers of China feeling more or less secure at night. China's intelligence network was as good as America's CIA or Britain's MI-6. In many ways, it was more effective. Deng's ministry was not subject to the kind of oversight practiced in the Western democracies.

Deng had a round face that seemed to wear a perpetual frown. For a Chinese, he had large ears that stuck out from the sides of his head. It had been a long time since anyone had dared make fun of those ears.

"I am not convinced this article is entirely true," Deng said. "It may be what the Western press is fond of calling a 'false flag.' On the other hand, there is no doubt that the assassin who murdered our ambassador was a member of Yun's Ministry of State Security."

"You are certain of this?" Zhang asked.

"Yes. Our asset in the American CIA confirms it. He has been positively identified."

"Yet you doubt the truthfulness of the report."

"I do not doubt the assassin's identity, but why would Chairman Yun do such a thing? Without our support, his regime will collapse. Why would he risk offending us in such a manner? It could only bring bad luck to him."

"Give me permission and I will bring much more than bad luck to our esteemed ally," General Liu said.

"This is a time for caution, General," Zhang said. "Like you, I am tempted to remove this annoying thorn in our side once and for all. But we must be aware of the consequences."

"You mean the Americans."

"That is exactly what I mean. If we annex North Korea, it will almost certainly mean war. The Americans are already unhappy with our actions in the South China Sea."

"That is our rightful area of control," Liu said. "The *gwai lo* will not risk nuclear war over fishing rights."

"No, but we both know that much more than fishing rights are involved."

"The Americans will not permit us to enter North Korea unopposed," Deng said. "Look what they did when Yun sank their submarine. They were angry and sent their Seventh Fleet in spite of his warnings about entering North Korean waters. That is a formidable force. If Yun had attempted to stop the rescue effort, they would have crushed him. They know he has nukes, but they chose to risk it."

"Even Yun wasn't stupid enough to take on the American Seventh Fleet," Liu said.

"He may not be stupid, but you are making the mistake of thinking he is rational," Deng said. "He is not. The man displays disturbing signs of mental disorder. He is delusional."

"Paranoid?"

Deng nodded, once. "The medications he takes support an assessment along those lines. Unfortunately, he does not take them as regularly as he should. If he had not agreed to the solution proposed by our Russian comrades, I believe war would have started. He would have attacked the American ships."

"Comrades?" Zhang looked amused.

"In a manner of speaking, in this particular instance."

"What do you propose?" Zhang asked. "We cannot let this pass unnoticed."

"*'A moment of patience in a moment of anger prevents a thousand moments of regret,'*" Deng said. "I need time to verify the truth or falsehood of this report."

"How will you begin?"

"I already have. Interestingly, the Korean murderer was recently treated here in Beijing for terminal cancer. My agents are questioning everyone who interacted with him. Perhaps the disease unhinged him and he acted on his own."

"That seems unlikely," Zhang said. "How did he get from Pyongyang to Washington? Where did he get the explosives he used?"

"You have mentioned two reasons why it is possible the report is true," Deng said.

"How much time do you need, Minister Deng?"

"A week should be sufficient."

"What if the report turns out to be accurate?" Liu asked.

"In that case, we will have to consider the best response."

"Yun should be eliminated."

"That may not be possible without starting a war with the West."

"Perhaps," Zhang said, "perhaps not. There is always more than one way to accomplish a goal."

CHAPTER 22

Nick's secured phone vibrated in his pocket as he pulled into the HQ parking lot. Elizabeth Harker was calling from her hospital bed.

"Good morning, Director. You're up early."

"Did you ever try to sleep late in a hospital?" Harker said. "They wake me up at four in the morning to give me a pill."

"What's up?"

"Have you checked the Internet this morning?"

"No, I just got here."

"There's a new video showing up everywhere, an interview with an anonymous source who claims to be a high-level defector from Russia. His face is obscured and his voice electronically masked in the video. It's impossible to identify him. The video was released by the same journalist who wrote about Chairman Yun's role in the assassination of the Chinese ambassador."

"What does this defector say?"

"That the assassination was planned in coordination with Washington."

"What? That's crazy."

"Not according to the man in the video. He says Moscow and the White House have made a secret agreement to ally against the PRC and that the file implicating Yun in the assassination is a false flag, cooked up to distract the Chinese from the real threat."

"And the threat is?"

"That Moscow and the White House are getting ready to go to war with China. According to the report, the assassination was the opening move. The journalist claims to have a copy of our war plans for China and says he's going to publish them."

"How the hell would a reporter get those?"

"I don't know, but he shows the first page in the video. It looks authentic."

"I wonder if the asshole who put this together gave any thought to how it would affect our relations with China, or national security? What's the matter with these people? We don't have an alliance with Russia against China, we both know that."

"I don't think truth matters much to the press, unless it supports the editor's point of view or improves the bottom line."

"That's a cynical statement."

"It's a cynical business," Harker said.

"China isn't going to like this."

"That may rank as the understatement of the year. See if you can find out what's going on."

"Something stinks about this," Nick said, "starting with the assassination. Why a suicide bomber? That's not the North Korean style."

"It was the style during the Korean War," Harker said. "They sent wave after wave of people carrying pitchforks and wearing not much more than quilted jackets against machine guns, knowing they'd be cut down."

"That was the Chinese, not the Koreans. They didn't have much of a choice with Mao running the show. This doesn't add up, Director. It's too neat. A North Korean agent throws himself on the ambassador's car, blows it up and himself with it. Then a computer turns up in his apartment with files on it identifying Yun as ordering the hit. Now we've got an anonymous Russian defector claiming it wasn't Yun after all, that the ambassador was killed as part of a larger plot by the U.S. and Russia against China."

"Go on."

"Put yourself in Chinese shoes. If I'm running the People's Republic, what am I supposed to think? Do I believe the story? Can I afford not to believe it? On a paranoia scale of one to ten, I'd say Beijing just hit twelve."

"It's true they're quick to think the worst," Harker said.

"According to what we've found out, the man who killed Li was a mid-level officer. Why would he have sensitive material about Yun on his computer? Right there, something's off. He wouldn't have access to that kind of information and I can't think of a single reason why it would be on his personal computer if he did."

"I've been wondering about that myself," Harker said.

"Now we have this video by a supposed defector, an anonymous source who comes out of the woodwork claiming there's a conspiracy against China. Why would he do that? Why now?"

"In the video, he states that he's doing it to prevent a war."

"I can't think of anything more likely to start one, if Beijing chooses to believe it."

In the background behind Harker, Nick heard the hospital speaker asking for someone to report.

"I want to question this guy," Nick said. "Someone put him up to this and provided him with at least part of our war planning about China. Whoever did it is guilty of treason. I'm thinking of Stephanie's AI computer. Freddie mentioned the possibility of a third party manipulating events."

"Freddie. I'd forgotten about him. Is Steph there yet?"

"Not yet."

"Go over this with her and have Freddie take a look at it. Let's see what he comes up with."

"If it is a third-party, what does he hope to gain?"

"Maybe he wants to start a war," Elizabeth said.

"That's insane. Why start a war that will end up going nuclear? Money? Ideology? Money isn't much good if there's nothing left to spend it on. Neither is ideology, if there's nobody left to control or convince."

"Track down the reporter. Talk to him. See if you can find out what's going on."

"Nice to have you back in charge, Director."

"You're still running things, Nick. I'm not out of here yet."

CHAPTER 23

The man who'd released the video was an independent investigative reporter named Michael Cotter who worked for anyone that would take his articles. The first report about Yun ordering the hit on the Chinese ambassador had brought him a lot of attention. With the video on Russia and Washington allying against China, he'd hit the big time. The interview had gone viral on social media and created a storm of controversy.

There were millions of people in the social media universe who had never been taught the critical skills of logical thinking required to understand what was false and what was not. Just because something was posted on Twitter or Facebook or showed up on the evening news didn't make it true. Now millions of people thought Moscow and Washington had formed a conspiracy against the Chinese. Some of those people were in China. It meant trouble.

There was no alliance between the U.S. and Russia against China, but the damage was done. Nick knew the interview was a lie, but the Chinese didn't. He wondered how they'd respond. He wasn't looking forward to finding out.

Someone was stirring up public opinion and poking sticks at the most dangerous players on the world stage. The animal that symbolized North Korea was a mythical, winged horse. It paled in significance compared to the dragon, bear, and eagle of the three great nuclear powers. If a war started between all of them, no one would survive.

Nick turned into the parking lot of the building at the address Stephanie had given him for the reporter.

"How's your stomach?" Nick asked.

That morning, Selena had been retching over the toilet.

"It's fine now. I think it must've been that restaurant we went to."

"I almost had the same thing you did," Nick said. "I thought that chicken you ate was a little off-color."

They pulled up in front of the reporter's building. The parking lot was cracked and potholed. Nick turned off the ignition.

"Not exactly high-end," Selena said.

Cotter lived in a forgettable three-story block of older apartments painted yellow. Small balconies with black iron railings jutted out from each unit, littered with bicycles, barbecues and plastic chairs. Rust streaks ran down the side of the building from the roof. A large, faded banner advertised two months free rent with move-in and a one-year lease.

Nick looked at the banner. "Doesn't look as though our journalist is living the high life."

"Stephanie did some research on him. He's got two ex-wives and big child support payments."

"Let's see if he's home."

They climbed an outside flight of concrete steps to Cotter's third floor unit. 3C was in the back of the building. The door to the unit was ajar.

"Would you leave your door unlocked around here?" Nick asked.

"No way. You might as well post a sign saying 'steal my stuff.'"

They drew their pistols and moved to opposite sides of the door. Nick reached out with the flat of his hand and gave the door a shove. It swung open. An unpleasant odor came from inside. Nick had smelled it often enough in the past.

The smell of death.

He risked a quick look around the doorframe. The front door opened onto a living room lit by daylight filtering through dirty windows. A hall went from the living room toward a kitchen/eating area in the back of the apartment. Nick could see an open doorway down the hall.

Selena gave him a questioning look. He nodded and stepped into the apartment, holding his Sig ready in both hands. Selena followed, steps behind.

The living room had a faded rug and an uncomfortable looking brown couch placed in front of a new large screen TV. The expensive TV felt out of place in an apartment like this. A cheap desk stood under the window. The drawers had been pulled out and the contents dumped on the floor. A disconnected power cord hinted at a missing computer.

The door off the hall led to a bedroom and bath. The bedroom had been searched, the dresser drawers emptied, the mattress cut open and tossed aside. The bathroom cabinet had been gone through.

They found Cotter in the kitchen, crumpled in a heap on the floor. He had a neat hole in his forehead. The hole wasn't so neat in back, where the bullet had exited. A large piece of his skull had been blown away. Most of his brain oozed from the wound. The rest was spattered over the refrigerator and the kitchen wall. Cotter wore a cheap suit and a shirt that had once been white. He wasn't wearing a tie.

Nick holstered his gun and bent down over the body. He touched Cotter's neck.

"Still warm. He probably never knew what hit him."

"Makes it hard to ask him anything," Selena said.

"I expect that was the point of killing him."

"This has to be related to the video."

"Someone didn't want him talking about where he got his information," Nick said.

Selena brushed her hand across her forehead. "This is getting complicated, isn't it?"

"It always does."

Nick stood, walked back down the hall and closed the open front door.

"If anything was here that could tell us something about that video, it's probably gone. We need to look anyway. You take the bedroom and bath, I'll start here."

While Selena began in the bedroom, Nick started going through the kitchen drawers and cabinets. All he found were dishes and cutlery. He opened the refrigerator, careful not to step in Cotter's blood. The freezer held a package of frozen burgers, three unopened boxes of frozen macaroni and cheese and a piece of pizza in a plastic bag. The main compartment held a few eggs, a stick of butter, and a carton of half-and-half going sour. Whatever else Cotter had been, he hadn't been a gourmet.

Selena came back into the room.

"Any luck?"

"Nothing," she said. "Just underwear and socks on the floor and a few things in the closet. He was taking Valium." She held up a prescription bottle. "Did you check the body?"

"I was just about to do that."

Nick checked Cotter's pockets, looking for a phone or a wallet. He rolled the body over.

"Well, well," Nick said. "Our investigative reporter was on the job."

He pulled out a small tape recorder that had been taped in the small of Cotter's back. He put it in his jacket pocket.

"He was wired," Selena said.

"Let's hope he was interviewing his killer. Let's get out of here."

"Suits me. My stomach is still a little uneasy. Looking at our friend here isn't helping."

They closed the door to the dead man's apartment and started down the steps to Nick's car.

He'd thought about getting something fancy, a Mercedes or maybe a BMW. In the end he'd opted for what felt familiar and settled on a Chevy Suburban. He'd taken it to the same specialist who'd modified Ronnie's Hummer. The big SUV boasted six hundred turbocharged horses and bulletproof glass, with steel plating around the engine compartment, inside the doors and around the gas tank. The truck was heavy and not especially agile, but it could move like hell when he opened it up.

It was painted black. Lamont called it the Bat Tank.

A bullet burned past Nick's head as he opened the driver side door. He registered the sound of the shot at the same time it smashed into the windshield on the passenger side. Instinct and training kicked in. He dropped to the ground and rolled under the car as a second round followed the first.

Selena was on the other side of the car, about to get in. She ducked down near the hood and spotted three men by a gray sedan across the parking lot. They fired at her. The rounds went over her head and struck a dumpster. She raised up and let off three quick shots, then crouched again behind the plated engine compartment.

Nick rolled out from underneath the car and came up beside her.

"Three of them," she said. "By a gray BMW." She pointed. "Pistols."

"At least…"

Whatever Nick was going to say was interrupted by a machine pistol opening up. Bullets peppered the suburban, making star-shaped patterns on the windows and punching into the bodywork on the other side of the car.

"At least what?"

"I was going to say, at least they don't have a machine gun."

They heard doors slam, then tires screeching. The gray sedan roared by them on the other side. The car fishtailed out of the parking lot and into the street.

Nick ran to the driver side and pulled open the door. It was stitched with bullet holes. Selena climbed in on the right as Nick started the engine. He pulled the wheel hard left and stepped on the gas, bouncing over the parking lot curb and onto the road. Ahead, the BMW accelerated away.

Star-shaped spots pockmarked the windshield where rounds had struck, but he could see well enough ahead to follow the shooters. They were in a part of the city that was a mix of industrial and residential. Traffic was light. They passed an outlet advertising tile and granite countertops. Nick put his foot down and the turbos cut in. The big Suburban began gaining on the car fleeing in front of them. They passed over a humped railroad crossing and left the ground, coming down hard.

Ahead, one of the shooters leaned out of a window and began firing. More stars appeared on the windshield.

Maybe an Uzi, Nick thought. *They keep that up, I won't be able to see where I'm going.*

Selena rolled down her window, reached out and fired four rounds. The man with the machine pistol jerked and slumped over the side of his door. His weapon flew out of his hand.

"Good shooting," Nick said.

They were coming up fast on a T-shaped intersection with a stop sign. Across the intersection stood a large ceramics factory that manufactured pots and containers. Hundreds of ceramic pots of varying sizes were stacked up in the yard in front of the building. Glazed pots of every color, plain clay pots, big and small pots, a pot for every fancy.

The sound of the turbos was a muted howl as they sped toward the intersection. Nick glanced at the speedometer. They were going over ninety and running out of road. A stream of traffic flowed by across the T ahead. Nick took his foot off the accelerator and hit the brakes hard. The car vibrated and juddered as the ABS kicked in.

Nick saw the BMW's brake lights go on, but the driver had left it too late. The car went through the stop sign and clipped the back of a pickup truck. Pieces of metal flew into the air. The BMW spun out of control, flipped, and rolled into the mesh fence separating the ceramics factory from the road. It flattened the fence, bounced into the air and landed in the pottery display.

The pots exploded into thousands of fragments, a chaotic, colorful shower that fountained high into the air. The BMW came to rest on its roof. Then it caught fire.

Nick drove across the intersection and brought the Suburban to a stop. Cars slowed to gawk at the burning wreckage..

"Maybe they're still alive," Selena said. "We should…"

The BMW exploded in bright, orange flame before she could finish her sentence.

"We should what?"

"Never mind," she said.

CHAPTER 24

Back at Project HQ, Nick gave Cotter's recorder to Stephanie. But when she played the recording, it was blank. Nick called Elizabeth and briefed her on what had happened. Selena and Stephanie listened to the conversation.

"We have to assume the men in that car were the ones who killed Cotter and searched his apartment," Nick said. "But why were they still at Cotter's building? If I'd just murdered someone, I wouldn't hang around."

"They could have been waiting for someone," Elizabeth said.

"How would they know someone would show up?"

My analysis indicates an eighty-nine point four percent possibility that they were waiting for you, Nick.

"Freddie. I didn't know you were listening."

I am always listening, unless I have been instructed not to.

"Okay, I'll bite. Why do you think they were waiting for us?"

I do not understand your reference to mastication.

"Freddie," Stephanie said, "I'll explain it later. Why do you think those people were waiting for Nick and Selena?"

Analysis of the video purporting to show a defecting Russian agent claiming that Washington and Moscow have formed an alliance against China reveals a unique technical signature consistent with the technology found in the camera used in the drone destroyed by Nick. Logically, whoever is responsible for sending the drone to spy on Project Headquarters is also responsible for the video.

According to that video, the assassination of the Chinese ambassador by a North Korean agent is a false flag designed to distract the Chinese from the supposed conspiracy between Washington and Moscow. The Project team was present at the assassination. Therefore, it is logical to assume that we would be involved in investigating that event. It is also logical to assume we would interview Cotter and try to determine where he had gotten his information.

Stephanie heard Freddie say "we" and realized that the computer's artificial intelligence had evolved to the point of identification with humans, at least with the members of the Project team. It was unexpected.

"Are you saying the same person who sent men to kill Cotter told them to wait for us to show up and ambush us?" Nick asked.

That is the logical conclusion.

Harker's voice came over the speaker phone. "Freddie, this is Elizabeth. I have a question."

Good morning, Director Harker. How are you feeling today?

"I'm fine, Freddie, thank you. Let me see if I understand what you're saying. You think that the same person who sent the drone also manufactured the false video."

That is correct.

"You also think this person knew we would want to talk to Cotter?"

That is correct.

"That still doesn't provide a reason to ambush us."

I do not have enough information to determine a reason.

"Who is this person?"

I do not have enough information to determine who is responsible.

"You said the technology used to create the video has a unique signature in common with the drone Nick destroyed."

That is correct.

"Can you perform a search for similar technology used in other applications?"

Yes.

"Good. Please do so. If we can find more examples, we might be able to trace them to the person responsible."

Processing.

"It doesn't make sense," Nick said. "I understand why someone might want Cotter out of the way. But why pick a fight with us?"

"And send a drone to attack us?" Elizabeth said.

"It feels personal," Selena said.

"Personal?" Nick looked at her. "Why do you think it's personal?"

"I don't know, it just does. Whoever it is must see us as a threat and thought we'd come looking for Cotter."

"They were right about that."

The light on Nick's phone for the line from Langley lit up. Nick answered.

"Nick, this is DCI Hood. We've identified the traitor who sent the plans for *Black Dolphin* to North Korea. He was an aide to General Samson of the Joint Chiefs."

"I'm putting you on speaker," Nick said. "You said he was an aide?"

"He's dead. He shot himself with a .45. It made quite a mess."

"Are you certain he's the one?"

"Yes. It gets worse. We think he also copied our war plan for China."

"That could explain how Cotter got his hands on it."

"I'm more concerned about China getting hold of it. The FBI is going through everything in Sanford's home and office as we speak, looking for anything that could lead us to his handler."

"Phone records?"

"His regular cell phone is clean. They found a throw away with calls in the phone log from different numbers, all disposable. It's probably a dead-end, but you never know. We're looking at his finances now. If there's an unusual amount of money, it might be traceable."

"Why did he do it?"

"We'll find out. At least the mole has been found and the leak stopped. You could even say that justice of a sort has been served."

"That's not much consolation to the families of the men who went down in that sub," Nick said.

CHAPTER 25

Supreme Leader Yun Chul-Moo felt the floor tremble under his feet as the hydrogen bomb detonated in its underground tunnel.

"Well?"

He turned to Park Moon, the man in charge of North Korea's nuclear program. Park stood in front of an array of instruments recording effects of the explosion. He was smiling.

"Great Leader, I am pleased to say that the test is an unqualified success."

"What is the yield?"

"Better than we expected. Four point two kilotons. Enough to register on the Western sensors, but they cannot be certain it was anything except an earthquake."

"Will *New Dawn* be ready in two weeks?"

New Dawn was the name Yun had given the EMP weapon he would use to attack the United States.

"The launch vehicle will be ready in days. *New Dawn* lacks only placement of the fissile material and the triggering mechanism. Before we install the final components, we need to move it to the launch site. We should be ready to launch within two weeks."

"And what will be the yield of the weapon?" Yun asked.

"Again, better than anticipated. Based on the result of this test, I estimate yield of *New Dawn* at between twenty-nine and thirty-two megatons."

"Excellent, Comrade Park. You have done well."

Yun snapped his fingers. An officer rushed forward and bowed, holding out a flat, black case. Yun opened the case and withdrew a medal. For a moment, Park looked confused. Then he came to attention.

"Comrade Park. You are awarded the Order of the National Flag, First Class, for achievements in scientific superiority in service to the nation."

Yun pinned the medal on Park's white laboratory smock. He began clapping.

The two dozen officers and lab workers present clapped loudly.

Park bowed. "I am unworthy of such an honor, Great Leader."

What would he have done if the test had failed? Park thought.

"Continue with your work, comrade. I am sure you will not fail us."

"Never, Great Leader." *Not if I want to stay alive.*

When Yun had left, Park turned to his chief engineer, standing nearby.

"You had better be right about the device being ready."

"Everything is on schedule, Director. Unless we run into an unforeseen problem, we will be ready on time. But I wish you had said a month rather than two weeks."

"Would you care to be the one to tell Chairman Yun that his weapon cannot be ready for him when he wants it? I told him what he wanted to hear."

The chief engineer nodded. "That is always the wisest course of action," he said.

"Prepare the device for shipment to Musudan-Ri."

The two men walked out of the control center. Neither one noticed the technician monitoring the radiation readouts who'd been listening to their conversation, nor had they seen the look of dismay on his face when he'd heard Park confirm the enormous yield of the weapon.

Cho Lee loved his country, but he loathed its leader. He knew enough about *New Dawn* to know it could lead to the destruction of everything he loved. Even if it were successful and the American homeland was destroyed, the Americans had powerful forces deployed in other parts of the globe. Their vengeance would be ferocious. They would obliterate the nation with their nuclear weapons.

Someone had to stop it from happening.

Radioactive fallout would spread over the borders with China and Russia. The Chinese didn't know what Yun was planning, but they were part of the problem. They kept him in power for their own ends. They couldn't be trusted to do what was right.

That left the Russians.

CHAPTER 26

Alexei Vysotsky watched Valentina come into his office and sit down.

She really is a beautiful woman. I envy Orlov.

"Before you start, be careful what you say," Valentina said.

"I take it you were successful?"

"If you can call it that."

"I didn't ask you here to talk about your dalliance," Vysotsky said, "though I admit, I am curious. We can leave that for another time. A problem is developing in Korea and we're going to have to do something about it."

"What problem?"

"That idiot who calls himself the Supreme Leader intends to set off a massive EMP explosion over North America."

"That's insane. The Americans have plenty of assets outside of their homeland that would not be affected. They will annihilate him, probably with nukes. It will lead to chaos. We'll be drawn in."

"Exactly. Major commands like the Seventh Fleet have orders to act independently if central command is knocked out. Once they knew Yun was responsible, they would retaliate."

"A nuclear attack on North Korea would cover us with fallout."

"You see, Valentina? This is one reason you are the perfect person for this operation. You understand the consequences of failure."

"You haven't said yet what the operation is."

"I want you to go into North Korea with a team and destroy Yun's launch vehicle. It would be better to stop him on the ground rather than trying to shoot his missile down. There is always a chance we would miss."

"An assault team is highly specialized. They will resent an outsider, especially a woman. Why do you want me to go with them?"

"I want to get Harker's group involved and I want you to act as liaison with them."

"Are you serious? You want to bring in the Americans my sister works with? Why?"

Vysotsky reached into his desk drawer and took out the bottle of vodka he always kept there, along with two glasses.

"Think it through, Valentina. She and her comrades have proven themselves exceptional in the field. They specialize in operations like this. Like you, they are highly trained and capable of independent operation. They adapt. They are ruthless. If they were Russian, they would be my first choice for this. Your sister speaks and reads Korean. You have worked together before. A certain level of trust exists between you."

"She is still an American," Valentina said.

"Did you know Arkady Korov?"

Vysotsky filled the glasses with vodka.

"I met him a few times."

"He was a fine officer, dedicated. It was a great loss when he was killed. For a while he worked closely with your sister's unit. He came to trust them. Once suspicion was dispelled, they accepted him as an equal. If we do this on our own and something goes wrong, it will be a public relations disaster. It could even lead to war. Yun's launch site is not far from China. If we try to shoot down his missile, it could be misinterpreted by Beijing. Plus there is more to consider."

"More?"

"Drink up."

They downed the vodka. Vysotsky told Valentina about the video claiming that Moscow and Washington had formed an alliance against China and were preparing for war.

"That's ridiculous," Valentina said. "It's obviously false."

"Obvious to us, perhaps. Not so obvious to the Chinese. My sources in Beijing inform me that the video created consternation at the highest levels."

"Are they really so naïve as to think we and the Americans would ally against them?"

"They are competing with us for resources and regional influence and are becoming annoyingly aggressive. There are many reasons for them to think we'd plot against them. It's what they do, and they expect the same of everyone else. The leadership is insecure. They see the Americans as an obstacle to their expansion in the China Sea and see us as looking for ways to recover what was lost in '89. They are correct on both counts. The idea that we would conspire against them fits their paranoid view of the world."

"We should just shoot the launch vehicle down," Valentina said. "I don't think we would miss."

"Perhaps not, but it runs the risk of provoking Beijing into doing something foolish. Shooting down the missile could push them over the edge. Yun would claim the launch was for peaceful purposes. A weather satellite, perhaps. China is his ally. It is a dangerous situation."

"I am not in favor of involving the Americans. Give me a *Spetsnaz* team and I will make sure this bomb never leaves the ground."

"What if the Americans have also learned of Yun's plan?" Vysotsky asked.

"If they've discovered what he's doing, they will try to stop him. Probably by sending in one of their covert units. One of their SEAL teams, perhaps."

"That is a safe assumption. Knowing the Americans, they will act sooner rather than later. What if they happen go in at the same time you are on the ground at the launch site?"

Valentina looked uncomfortable. "It would be difficult to avoid conflict."

"Which is another reason I would prefer to make sure there are no misunderstandings," Vysotsky said. "We do not need an incident between our two countries at this time, especially on North Korean territory. It is a reason to seek an alliance with your sister's unit. Better to work with the devil we know."

"How do you plan to involve them?" Valentina asked.

"Leave the Americans to me."

CHAPTER 27

Elizabeth sat in a chair by her hospital bed, dressed in a light blue robe, reading a book about the Revolutionary War. It was a time in American history she found fascinating. She was due to be discharged today or tomorrow, pending final clearance from her doctors. As far as she was concerned, it couldn't happen soon enough.

The secure phone resting in the pocket of her robe vibrated against her thigh. She took it out and looked at the display. The number was unfamiliar.

"Yes," she said. "Who is this?"

"Director. I am sure you recognize my voice. Is this line secure?"

Vysotsky. I'll be damned.

"General. Yes, the line is secure. To what do I owe this unexpected pleasure?"

"Always the diplomat, Elizabeth. It is one of the things I appreciate about you. I trust you are healing well?"

"Better, thanks. But this isn't a social call, is it?"

"I have some intelligence I wish to share with you, and I have a proposition."

"Intelligence is always welcome. If it is legitimate. I reserve judgment on the proposition."

"Elizabeth. You hurt my feelings. I would not insult you by attempting to give you false information. You are exposed to enough of that through your newspapers and politicians."

"As are you, General."

"Are you aware that Chairman Yun has developed a hydrogen bomb?"

"We suspect he is ready to test a small device."

"More than ready. He tested it this morning and it was successful."

"I didn't know that. That's bad news."

"And if I told you that he has built a much larger bomb, one modeled on our own Tsar Bomba?"

Elizabeth sat up straighter in her chair. "That would be worse news. But our sources say he doesn't have enough material for that kind of weapon."

"You underestimated his production, but you are correct that it was not enough. Yun obtained the rest of the plutonium and other fissile material he needed from Iran."

"Those fanatics in Tehran never give up, do they? What does he intend to do with this monster bomb?"

"He intends to set it off, of course. Three hundred miles above your country. I don't need to tell you what that would mean."

"You are certain of this?"

"I am."

Elizabeth was silent. How much should she tell Vysotsky?

"Director Harker? You are still there?"

"Yes, General. I was thinking. We knew Yun was working on a thermonuclear device," she said. "We've just discovered that he's developed a solid fuel engine for his missiles. It gives him ICBM capability. Our assumption has been that he plans to attack a Western target, either our own West Coast or possibly Japan. But if he has a bomb like you are talking about, that changes things."

"We were unaware Yun had progressed so far with his missiles," the Russian said.

"Then we've both learned something by this conversation," Elizabeth said. "His new engine was spotted installed on a modified Taepodong 2 missile. We don't think he's completely worked out the guidance system issues. He can send one up, but he can't necessarily put it where he wants it."

"He doesn't need an accurate ICBM for what he plans. He intends to place his bomb in orbit above you by using one of his satellite launch vehicles."

"You are sure your information is accurate?" Elizabeth asked again.

"Yes. It comes from someone in their nuclear program who overheard Yun talking about what he planned to do. He believes that if Yun goes through with his plan, you will retaliate with nuclear weapons and destroy his country. He wants us to stop it before it happens. I agree with him. Such an event could easily lead to war between all of us. The Chinese would not stand by if you attacked North Korea."

"Why go to you? Why not the Chinese?"

"He doesn't trust the Chinese. Yun is their ally."

"No one trusts the Chinese," Elizabeth said. "You mentioned a proposition. What did you have in mind?"

"We must prevent Yun from launching. I propose a joint operation to remove the threat. We've worked together before, to good effect. It's odd, isn't it? How these things come up from time to time which are more important than the enmity between our two nations? "

"There's nothing like a madman with a bomb to bring people together," Elizabeth said. "We didn't know about his plan, but we'd already decided we couldn't risk him launching a nuclear missile. The

President wants to take out the launch site before it can happen. We weren't certain which one to target."

"The EMP device is being transported to Musudan-Ri for the launch. It's the only option. His other site at Sohae is undergoing renovations to prepare for larger missiles. Our satellites show that the launch vehicle has not yet been moved onto the pad. We still have time to destroy it."

"Forgive me for asking, General, but your special forces are perfectly capable of doing this job on their own. Why do you want to involve us?"

"We are anxious to avoid misunderstandings," Vysotsky said. "I assumed your intelligence services would learn Yun had developed a hydrogen bomb. It makes sense someone would be sent to intervene. Politicians being the way they are, such a mission would have to be completely deniable. It seemed a good bet you would be aware of it. I had even anticipated that your unit might be chosen, as you've just confirmed. I don't want my assault team running into yours and making a mistake. The officer I have chosen to oversee the operation is well known to you. Her sister is on your team."

"Valentina? You're putting her in charge?"

"A Spetsnaz officer will be in charge of the combat team. Valentina will be in overall command and act as liaison between our two units. She has demonstrated her competence in difficult situations. She's the logical choice."

"I need to discuss this with the others," Elizabeth said, "but I will consider it. The logistics could get complicated."

"I can make staging facilities available on the Kamchatka Peninsula. It's not far from the target."

"How much time do I have to prepare? Assuming I agree."

"The sooner the better," Vysotsky said. "Yesterday would be good."

CHAPTER 28

Selena finished throwing up breakfast, stood, and flushed the toilet. She went to the bathroom sink and rinsed out her mouth.

I can't be, she thought. *It's not possible.*

"You okay?" Nick called from the other room.

"Fine," she called out. "I'll be right there."

She looked at herself in the mirror and saw nothing unusual staring back at her, no indication anything had changed. But she knew something had. She'd stop by the pharmacy later and pick up a test. There was no point in talking about it with Nick until she knew for certain.

She came out of the bathroom.

"What's going on?"

"I think I picked up a stomach bug, maybe a touch of flu. It's giving me a headache."

She did have a headache, but it wasn't because she thought she had flu.

Nick said, "We have to plan the mission."

"I'll be fine. Stop by a drugstore and I'll pick up some aspirin."

"There's a big pharmacy in that shopping center we pass on the way in. They'll have whatever you need."

Yes, they will.

"We'd better get going," Nick said.

At the shopping center, Nick waited in the car while Selena went inside. She bought two pregnancy tests and a small bottle of aspirin. Walking back to the car, she hoped she was wrong. Her mind sorted through scenarios where she was pregnant, with no good result. She was glad when they arrived at Project HQ. It meant she could turn her attention to something impersonal, something she understood.

The team waited for the briefing to begin. Nick settled in at Elizabeth's desk as his phone indicated a call from her.

"Morning, Director."

"Good morning, Nick. I'm being discharged today. More accurately, I'm discharging myself. But that's not the only reason I'm calling. I had a conversation a few minutes ago with General Vysotsky."

"Vysotsky? What did he want?"

Elizabeth told him. Then she said, "Vysotsky has made Selena's sister responsible for overseeing their end of the operation."

"Valentina? You're kidding."

"No, I'm not. We're going to have to coordinate the mission with the Russians. I want you to call Vysotsky and begin the process."

"Shouldn't we wait until you get back?"

"I'll be here for a few hours yet. The doctors insist on another bank of tests before they'll let me go. We need to get on this right away."

"All right."

Elizabeth gave Vysotsky's contact information to Nick.

"I'll be there as soon as I can. Get ready to go to Korea. While you're doing that, I need to clear this with the President."

"Copy that, Director."

He set the phone down on the desk. Everyone was looking at him.

"What's that about Valentina and Vysotsky?" Selena said.

"Harker just talked to him. It seems our good friend Chairman Yun plans to put a hydrogen bomb into orbit over us and set off an EMP explosion. A big one."

"That would wipe out the grid," Ronnie said.

"That guy is a looney tune," Lamont said.

"Vysotsky wants us to form a joint mission with one of their *Spetsnaz* teams and take out Yun's rocket before he can launch. Harker wants me to call him. Valentina is going to be in command of the Russians."

"Oh, that's just great," Selena said.

"Why are the Russians warning us about it?" Lamont asked. "They'd be happy to see us taken off the board."

"If that bomb goes off, Vysotsky thinks we'll retaliate with a nuclear strike on North Korea. He's worried it would lead to war with China, and that Russia would be dragged in."

"He's right," Ronnie said. "We'd hit them with everything we had."

"He's also right it would lead to war with China," Selena said. "Russia couldn't escape getting caught up in it. No one would win."

"We have a firm target. Vysotsky told Harker the bomb is going to be launched from Musudan-ri."

Musudan-ri is no longer known by that designation. It has been renamed Tonghae.

"Whatever it's called, we're going to destroy it. Freddie, bring up a map of the region and satellite photos of the target."

The map and pictures appeared on the monitor screen. The launch facility was located in the northeast of the country, a short distance inland from the Sea of Japan and not far from the

Kamchatka Peninsula, near Vladivostok. The area surrounding the launch site was gently rolling, sparsely populated, and covered with snow.

"Sure wish this target was somewhere warm," Lamont said.

"Not exactly Cape Canaveral," Ronnie said.

"By our standards it's primitive, but it's good enough for them to put a satellite into orbit." Nick took a laser pointer off the desktop and clicked it on. The red dot moved across the screen.

"I took a look at this yesterday, when we weren't sure which of their sites would be the target. You can see the launch pad and the gantry and tower next to it. That road leading away to the south goes to launch control, this building here."

The laser dot moved.

"This small building with the radar tower is the control station for their anti-aircraft missile batteries. The low buildings to the west are assembly sheds. They built a new addition not long ago. It's a little over thirty meters long. That's the exact height of the launch tower. Their rocket is still in that building."

He moved the pointer.

"This construction over here is for a new, larger facility. Those structures don't concern us. Our target is the assembly building and the tower. If the rocket is already on the launch pad, we forget about the assembly building."

"What's that building in the lower left corner of the picture?" Selena asked.

"I was going to talk about that next. It's a barracks for a company of special forces soldiers. Mostly they patrol the road coming in from the coast. They're under strength but we don't want to tangle with them."

"When were these pictures taken?" Ronnie asked.

These photographs were taken twelve hours, thirty-four minutes and six seconds ago.

"How long does it take to set up and fuel?" Selena asked.

Positioning the rocket for launch and fueling takes approximately two days.

"We need a more recent shot," Lamont said.

Accessing.

Seconds later a new shot of the launch site appeared on the monitor. This picture showed a transporter hauling a long, shrouded shape from the assembly building.

The size and shape of the covered launch vehicle in the photo suggests that it is an Unha-3. It is a three stage rocket used in the past by the North Koreans to place weather satellites in orbit. It must be fueled shortly before launch and is highly unstable.

"I don't see any permanent fueling facility," Lamont said. "They must bring in fuel with tankers."

"We can target the trucks," Ronnie said. "They're bombs on wheels."

"Ought to make a hell of a bonfire," Lamont said.

"We have to get on site first," Nick said.

"Russia isn't far from the target," Selena said. "It would be easier to stage from there than from Japan."

Nick fiddled with the pointer. "Until I talk with the Russians we can't pin down details. But we can get the logistics ready. It's cold over there right now. You three put together what we need for personal gear. Pack one of our AT-4's. Take plenty of C4 and our own detonators. The Russians will have theirs but I want to work with our own stuff."

"When are we leaving?" Selena asked.

"The target's on the other side of the world. Plan on wheels up early tomorrow."

CHAPTER 29

Vladimir Orlov listened to General Vysotsky explain his plan. Pale winter sunlight streamed through the windows of Vladimir Orlov's Kremlin office, the kind of light that cast no warmth.

"You should have come to me before you contacted Harker," Orlov said.

"I apologize, Mister President. I wanted to be sure she would cooperate before I informed you. Our interactions with them in the past have been successful. It's an unusual situation, I admit, but common threats have made them useful allies in the past."

"This is the unit with Colonel Antipov's half-sister."

"Yes. Because of this, I want Colonel Antipov to command."

"As you are aware, she is not experienced in this kind of operation. Her skills are somewhat different."

"Yes, sir. Her second-in-command will be Major Vasiliev. He is an experienced Spetsnaz officer with extensive combat experience. I have instructed Colonel Antipov to defer to him in the field."

Orlov snorted. "Colonel Antipov does not strike me as someone who is likely to defer to anyone."

"I agree, but she will follow orders. She is the perfect officer to act as liaison with the Americans. It will help us avoid problems with them."

"Has Yun mounted his bomb on the launch vehicle?"

"We don't think so, but it's possible. We haven't seen anything to indicate that the bomb is on site but they've moved the rocket to the tower. It has not yet been placed in position. Once it's in position, we can be certain the missile is armed. Our source in Korea said there was a two week window to launch. That was ten days ago. Perhaps we have four days, but I want to destroy the facility as soon as possible."

"You are certain we need the assistance of the Americans."

"We don't need their assistance, Mister President, but I think we must include them. They believed Yun intended to launch a missile with a nuclear warhead and had decided to send in a covert team and destroy his facility. There could have been an incident if our forces and the Americans showed up at the same time. Better to work together for the common goal, than risk the possibility of confrontation and failure."

"Very well, you may proceed. Be sure there is nothing pointing back to us if things go wrong."

"There will be no indications we were ever there, Mister President."

"I am holding you personally accountable for the success of this mission."

"Yes, sir."

In other words, if things go wrong your next assignment will be in Siberia, Vysotsky thought. *He's not going to like what I tell him next.*

"There's another problem, Mister President."

Orlov gave Alexei a sour look. "What is it?"

"Since the elimination of Minister Sirco, Kiev has been stirring up the American press with rumors that we intend to invade."

"That's nothing new. The American press is irresponsible. We are not ready for a ground war in Ukraine, not after the Balkan fiasco."

The year before, Orlov had been tricked into believing he could invade the Baltic States without NATO response. It had almost started World War III. The Russian forces had retreated at the last moment.

"Just the same, I have learned that the Americans have started deploying their so-called 'European Missile Shield' in the Western region. It's a shore based version of their Aegis defense system."

Orlov's face tightened.

"They are being stupid. They know we can't let them place missiles so close to our borders. It is a deliberate provocation."

"Especially since we could easily destroy the emplacements."

"Sometimes I think it is their intention to begin a war with us."

"That is a war they would not win."

"No," Orlov said, "they would not. But neither would we."

"We must respond to their actions."

"Do not worry, General. Since they threaten us with force, we will do the same. I will order our SS-20 intermediate-range missiles deployed along the border. They threaten us, we will threaten Europe. Two can play the game."

"Those missiles are forbidden by treaty," Vysotsky said.

"Treaties are meant to be broken," Orlov said.

CHAPTER 30

China had many ears in North Korea. Word of Yun's plan to attack America had reached Beijing. There were unhappy senior officers in Yun's country, men who feared the next purge would remove them from their privileged positions of power. The execution of Admiral Hwan had sent shockwaves through the top ranks of the North Korean military. Hwan had been a respected and trusted officer. If the Chairman could turn on him, who would be next? One of those officers had made sure their Chinese ally knew of Yun's folly.

A decision had to be made. President Zhang Jei sipped tea while General Liu and Minister Deng waited for him to speak. Zhang set his cup down and dabbed at his lips with a linen cloth.

"It is tempting to allow the destruction of our enemy," Zhang said, "but *'Temptation wrings integrity, even as the thumbscrew twists a man's fingers.'*"

"*'It is on the path you do not fear, that the wild beast catches you',*" Deng said. "It is certainly tempting. But if we allow Yun to destroy the American homeland, they will retaliate. They've based their nuclear weapons around the world, preparing for just such a contingency. They will be angry and turn North Korea into a wasteland. Angry people make mistakes. It will mean war, a war we cannot hope to win."

"I fear that Chairman Yun has reached the end of his usefulness as an ally," Zhang said. "More tea, General?"

Without waiting for a response, Zhang filled General Liu's cup.

"We cannot allow him to launch," Liu said.

"I agree. How do you think we should proceed?"

"I can place a South Blade unit on site. They will destroy his rocket before he can put it in the air."

Deng nodded. "A sensible solution. Afterward, we can deal with Yun."

"Are there any rules of engagement?" Liu asked.

"No one must know we were there," Zhang said. "Take any action necessary. If there is opposition, eliminate it."

"Prisoners might provide useful intelligence," Deng said.

"There is no provision for prisoners on an operation like this," Liu said.

"It doesn't have to be complicated," Deng said. "If you take prisoners, interrogate them and then kill them."

Liu grunted assent.

"How much time do you need for preparation, General?" Zhang asked.

"It requires some thought, but two days should be adequate. We need to study the target, brief the mission, and arrange logistics."

"We must make sure the weapon is destroyed," Deng said. "It's not enough to eliminate the launch facility. The bomb would not have been manufactured at the launch site. Yun will have to move it from wherever it is, install it on the launch vehicle, and make final adjustments."

"Establish twenty-four hour surveillance. General Liu, once we are certain the bomb has been moved to Musudan-Ri, send in your team."

"What about afterward?"

"What do you mean, General? Extraction of our forces? Surely, you can handle that."

"Not extraction, Mister President. I meant Yun. What are we going to do about him?"

"Chairman Yun will be very angry," Zhang said. "He will probably have one of his fits. Alas, such things are unpredictable. I have heard that the effects on one's health can be quite serious, even fatal."

CHAPTER 31

"I'm going to call Vysotsky," Nick said. "I'll put it on speaker, but I'd ask everyone to remain quiet. Especially you, Freddie."

As you wish.

It was odd to call up a Russian general, much less the director of Russia's foreign intelligence service. Speaking politely with one of America's principle enemies was something new in Nick's experience.

He's a smoothie, Harker had told him once. *You can only trust him so far.*

Nick entered Vysotsky's number on his satellite phone. The voice that answered was rough-hewn.

"Da."

"General Vysotsky, this is Nicholas Carter, acting for Director Harker. She has asked me to speak with you and coordinate our mission together."

"Major Carter. I have heard much about you. You and your team are well known here. Major Korov spoke highly of you."

"Arkady Korov was an outstanding officer," Nick said. "He had become a friend."

"Different uniforms are not always a barrier to friendship," Vysotsky said. "Circumstances can create alliances where none existed before."

"As seems to be the case again."

"As in the past, we find ourselves facing a common threat. Did Director Harker explain why I proposed a joint mission? Why I feel it's the best option?"

"She did. Since neither one of us would consider standing down regarding Yun, I agree it's best to avoid any possibility of an incident between us."

"Good. I have spoken with President Orlov and he has given his blessing to the operation. You will be permitted to bring your team and weapons into our airspace. The nearest airbase to our objective is Petropavlosk-Kamchatsky, near Vladivostok."

"One moment, General. Let me pull up a map of the area."

Stephanie tapped on her keyboard. The map appeared.

"We can come in from Misawa Air Force Base in Japan," Nick said. "It's close, about five hundred miles by air."

"Be sure to let me know when you are about to take off," Vysotsky said. "Our air defense forces are efficient."

"Tell me what you have in mind, General. I understand that Colonel Antipov will be in command of your unit. Is that correct?"

Valentina was in Vysotsky's office, listening to the conversation.

"That is correct. She is here with me now. Is your team present at your end?"

"They are."

"Excellent. Valentina, say hello to your sister."

Valentina rolled her eyes. "Sister. You are well?"

Selena hadn't expected to hear Valentina's voice. "I am. And you?"

"It seems we will be seeing each other soon," Valentina said.

"There are things we should talk about," Selena said.

"If you wish. If there's time."

Vysotsky said, "Major Carter, how soon can you be here?"

"Thirty-six hours, tops. Possibly less."

"What is your information on the status of Yun's weapon?"

"We have the target under continuous satellite surveillance," Nick said. "So far, we do not believe the bomb has been brought to the site. Once it's there, we estimate a day to install it on the launch vehicle, then two days to prepare for launch. We still have a little time."

"That agrees with our own estimates. Once you arrive, we will have a detailed joint briefing. Valentina's second-in-command is one of my best officers, Major Vasiliev. He will be in charge of the assault. Colonel Antipov will be in overall command of the mission."

"I don't have a problem with your people being in charge," Nick said, "but we need to discuss it. I'm sure you're aware that clear boundaries of command in an operation like this are critical. If we get into a pissing match, it won't do anyone any good."

"You are direct, Major Carter."

"I would suggest that Major Vasiliev and myself maintain control of our individual units under Colonel Antipov's overall command. I have great respect for your special forces units. I have no doubt Major Vasiliev is a professional, but I am uncomfortable handing over tactical placement of my team to someone I haven't met or worked with in the past."

Valentina looked at Vysotsky as if to say *I told you so*.

"Very well. We will discuss it once you are here. Inform me when you leave Washington, and again when you are ready to leave Japan. The number you have will reach me anytime of the day or night."

"Will you be conducting the briefing?"

"I wouldn't miss it for anything," Vysotsky said.

CHAPTER 32

The Gulfstream assigned to the Project was down for maintenance. They hitched a ride on a C-17 from Andrews to Misawa Air Force Base in Japan. From there they'd transfer to a smaller plane for the flight to Petropavlosk-Kamchatsky airport in Russia.

Selena did her best to get comfortable on the orange strap bench that passed for seating in the cavernous hold of the plane. She wore a white camouflage uniform with scattered gray and tan colored patterns. In almost any winter environment, she would be invisible. Thermal underwear, gloves, and a balaclava that covered her face in the same camouflage pattern meant she would stay reasonably warm. The outfit kept her comfortable in the hold of the C-17.

Her field pack and a suppressed MP-7 were stored by her feet. A pistol was holstered on her chest and a fighting knife strapped to her thigh. The plane, the boredom of the journey, the pack at her feet, the weapons of death strapped on her body were all too familiar, something she'd gotten used to since she'd joined the Project. Everything was the same as usual.

Except everything had changed.

Selena's mind was in turmoil. The pregnancy tests had been positive. She didn't know why her birth control had failed, but it was a moot point. She wasn't showing, yet. Morning sickness usually started about six weeks in, too soon for any outward indication. She listened to the monotonous drone of the engines and thought about the life growing inside her.

She hadn't told Nick yet. She'd rationalized that she didn't want to distract him before the mission, but the truth was that she didn't know how he was going to handle it. Hell, she wasn't certain how *she* was going to handle it.

She was thirty-nine years old and set in her ways. A baby meant upheaval. She wasn't even sure she could have a safe pregnancy or bring a child to term. She'd taken serious wounds in the past few years, wounds that had torn up her insides and almost killed her. A round from an AK-47 had taken out one of her ovaries. It was a miracle she could walk, much less conceive.

I have to tell him. After the mission, when we get back.

When she'd been younger, she'd thought about having children. Her drive for personal independence and the fact that she hadn't met anyone she trusted as a potential father of her children had combined to make her put off the decision. As the years passed, she'd thought about it less and less.

That was a luxury she no longer had.

She heard the pitch of the engines change. Nick had been talking with Ronnie. Now he came over and sat down next to her.

"We're in the landing pattern for Misawa," he said. "We'll be on the ground in half an hour."

"I'll be glad to get off this damn bench."

Nick laughed. "All these years, they haven't changed much. You never quite get used to them."

"I'm not looking forward to this," she said.

"Because of Valentina?"

"That's part of it. Maybe even most of it. I don't like the idea that we're not in charge. I trust you. I don't trust her, or the Russians."

"It worked out all right with Korov."

"Yes, but he proved himself to us, didn't he?"

"So has your sister. She saved your butt in Germany. If she hadn't acted in Egypt, we'd all be dead."

"I suppose so."

"Where we're going, we're all on the same side," Nick said.

"What if that bomb goes off when we blow it up?"

"It can't. The way a hydrogen bomb works requires a controlled sequence of events. You have to set off a smaller, atomic explosion that acts to start the reaction. It's a staged event. The first fission explosion triggers a second, larger one. A big bomb might require a third stage as well. But it all has to happen in an exact manner. Just blowing it up won't set it off."

"Why didn't we suspect that he was so far advanced with the technology?"

"I don't know. I think people assumed his facilities and resources were too limited. He's good at hiding things."

"I can't shake the feeling that something is going to go wrong."

"It's just pre-mission jitters, that's all. Once we're in the field, you'll be fine. You always have been in the past. This time is no different."

Yes, it is, she thought.

CHAPTER 33

Nick called Vysotsky from Misawa Air Force Base as they were about to leave. Their ride was a C-23 cargo plane, an odd looking, propeller driven aircraft with stubby wings and a large, double tail. It was designed for transporting small combat units and their equipment over an operational theater. It wasn't particularly fast and it wasn't designed for comfort.

Unlike the flight that had brought them to Japan, this plane had windows. That was the only thing it had in common with a regular passenger plane. It didn't have a bathroom, only a tube to urinate in. Women didn't usually fly in a C-23. There was no heat in the main cabin and no pressurization. The plane was painted green and looked as if it had been dreamed up during an aircraft engineer's hangover.

They took off into a gray sky that promised snow.

Some time later, Selena pointed out the window.

"We have company."

Outside the plane, a Russian fighter pulled up a hundred feet away and held station. She could see the pilot and the weapons officer seated behind him.

"This side, too," Ronnie said.

"Must be hard for them to keep station, going slow like this," Lamont said.

"That's a Mig-31," Nick said. "NATO calls it the Foxhound. As good as anything we've got. Fast and lethal. Take a look at those missiles under the wings."

"That's as close a look as I ever want to get," Lamont said.

In a little while the Kamchatka Peninsula appeared, a finger sticking out into the Sea of Japan. The airport was surrounded by tall, snowcapped mountains and extinct volcanoes. It was literally at the end of nowhere, a far-flung outpost of a fragmented Empire, so isolated that there were no roads leading to the capital city of two hundred thousand people. It was only accessible by air.

Their fighter escort peeled away as they approached the runway. Two armored vehicles with top mounted heavy machine guns and a command car pulled alongside as they landed. The vehicles fanned out to either side and kept pace with the plane. A soldier stood in the back of the car and waved to the pilot to follow him. The plane taxied past a terminal building that looked as though it had been built in the 1950s and kept going until they entered the military section of the airport.

They passed a dozen of the Mig-31's, parked in neat rows within hardened revetments. Everything was precisely organized, professional looking. Except for the archaic terminal building, the planes, and the insignia on them, they could have been on a base somewhere in America.

"Serious base," Ronnie said.

"The Russians are serious people," Nick said. "Anyone who buys into the myth that their military is falling apart is out of their minds. It used to be true, but not anymore. Not since Orlov took over."

The plane came to a halt. The cargo door in the back opened and dropped onto the tarmac. The pilot came out of the cabin. The name badge on his uniform said Kaplan.

"Thanks for flying the scenic Russian route," he said. "You may now exit through the rear. Enjoy your stay."

"Nice flight, Captain," Nick said.

Captain Kaplan looked at the four of them and the weapons they were carrying.

"I don't suppose y'all are here for a vacation," he said. "Take care of yourselves out there."

"Copy that," Nick said.

They descended the ramp onto Russian soil. A chill wind blew around them. The air smelled of coming snow.

General Vysotsky, Valentina, and a hard looking man about Nick's height waited for them.

Vysotsky was in full uniform, impressive with the stars on the shoulder boards of his heavy greatcoat and the red stripes on his trousers. He looked like what he was: a man who controlled a far-flung empire of spies and special forces units, a man you wouldn't want to cross. Valentina and her companion were dressed in winter camouflage uniforms not unlike what Nick and his team were wearing.

Vysotsky greeted Nick with a jovial smile. "Major Carter. I am pleased to meet you. You already know Valentina. This is Major Vasiliev."

Vasiliev didn't look particularly pleased to meet them, but it was difficult to tell what the Russian was thinking. He had the look that came with military life at the sharp end of the sword, the appearance of a professional warrior. He was about six feet tall, perhaps two hundred pounds. His face was square jawed, blunt, with a prominent nose. His hair was cropped close to his skull. Nick guessed he was somewhere in his late thirties.

Nick held out his hand. "Major. I'm looking forward to working with you."

Vasiliev hesitated, then took Nick's hand. His grip was strong, almost uncomfortable. Nick resisted the urge to overmatch him.

"I am sure it will be interesting."

Vasiliev's English was clear but accented.

"Follow me," Vysotsky said. "I have transportation waiting to take you to your quarters. You can drop your gear there. Briefing after that."

The Russians working on the base gave them curious looks as they walked to the bus Vysotsky had commandeered. Their accommodations were in the officers' barracks on the other side of the base.

Their rooms were the same as transient military quarters everywhere, minimal, equipped with the basics of a bed, a small table and a narrow closet for hanging uniforms. A tiny sink completed the facilities. A window looked out at the spectacular mountains surrounding the base. Bathrooms and showers were at the end of the hall.

They left their packs and MP-7s in the rooms. The building was stuffy, overheated against the cold. Nick was sweating by the time they got to the briefing room where Vysotsky and the other Russians waited.

A large map of North Korea took up most of the front wall. A half dozen satellite shots of the target area were pasted up on one side of the map. Two rows of hard wooden chairs faced the front of the room. The Russians sat in the front row. Nick and the others took seats.

"There are some new developments," Vysotsky said. "The transport vehicle with the bomb has arrived on the launch site. We estimate a minimum of one day to install the weapons package and make final adjustments. It would not have been transported in operational mode. Meanwhile, they'll be getting the launch vehicle ready. Tankers are on site and waiting."

"What about the weather?" Nick asked. "What's the forecast?"

"A front is moving in that may delay the launch. That's good, but it means the insertion will be more difficult."

"How do you plan to get us on site?" Ronnie asked.

"There have always been two options. Originally we were planning on insertion over the water. The target is not far from a fishing village named Tongha-Dong."

"Originally?"

"The weather will make that impossible. You don't want to be in an open boat on the Sea of Japan when one of our Arctic fronts moves in. Waves can be forty feet high out there."

"What's the second option?" Nick asked.

"Two of our MI-35MS helicopters. You and your team will go in one, Major Vasiliev and Colonel Antipov in the other."

"Excuse me, General, but how do you propose avoiding North Korean radar? Our intelligence indicates that Yun has excellent defensive surveillance facilities, courtesy of his Chinese allies."

"Are you concerned for your safety, Carter?" Vasiliev said.

Asshole, Nick thought. *He's going to be trouble.*

"I'll choose not to take that as an insult, Major. I am concerned for the success of the mission. So I ask again, how do you propose to avoid the Korean defenses?"

"A reasonable question," Vysotsky said. "The MI-35MS is a new design, equipped for stealth operations. It's a variation on our first-line attack helicopter, quiet and almost invisible to conventional radar. It's also well armed with several types of missiles, a double twenty-three millimeter cannon, and antimissile defenses. It is somewhat better than similar American machines."

Ronnie raised his eyebrows at the comment. Vysotsky continued.

"It can reach a maximum speed of over three hundred kilometers an hour and is equipped to fly at night over water at a height of twenty meters."

"What if it's snowing?"

"If it's snowing, that is not a problem. From here you will head south over the Sea of Japan, then make a quick turn in toward the target. I am confident you will not be spotted."

He turned to the map. "Major Vasiliev has designated a landing zone here, five kilometers from the target. He feels this will minimize the risk of detection." He tapped a point on the map. "From there you will proceed overland to the site. When the target has been destroyed, you will return to the LZ for exfiltration."

Nick raised his hand.

"You have a comment?" Vysotsky looked annoyed.

"Five klicks is a long way to go, especially if the weather is bad."

"How would you do it, Major Carter?"

"Normally, I'd say go in hot and hit them before they know what's happening. With their defenses, that's not an option. My concern is that five klicks is a long way to go back to the LZ after stirring up that hornet's nest. We should land closer to the target."

Vasiliev snorted. "Perhaps a run of five kilometers after the assault is beyond your ability? My troops can be back at the LZ before the North Koreans recover. It is foolish to risk possible detection by flying in closer as you suggest."

"Foolish? It's more than foolish to wake up the North Korean defenses and hope to make it back five kilometers before they crank up their missiles and interceptors. Unless you think your stealth technology isn't good enough to get close."

Vasiliev's face turned red. "Our helicopters are the best in the world. Our cloaking technology is superior."

"It had better be, or we won't even get as close as five klicks," Nick said. "When we hit that target, the whole sky is going to light up with the fireworks. How long do you think it will take before reinforcements show up? How long before someone talks to the missile batteries? How long before they scramble fighters from the nearest base? I don't care if your people can make it back five klicks in five minutes. It's too far. Doing it that way turns this into a suicide mission."

"You overestimate the enemy capability," Vasiliev said.

"Bullshit. Their leader may be bat shit crazy, but he spares no expense equipping his military. Underestimating the enemy's capability or competence would be a serious mistake. We need to plan this mission accordingly."

Valentina and General Vysotsky had been watching the exchange. Now Vysotsky said, "Colonel Antipov. What is your opinion?"

Vasiliev stood. "With all due respect, General, Colonel Antipov is not familiar with this kind of field operation. This kind of planning requires experience."

"Major, you need to remember who is in command here. Sit down."

Vysotsky just handed Vasiliev his ass in a sling. He's not going to forget that, Nick thought. *This is a bad start.*

Vasiliev sat. His face was red and tight.

"Both Major Vasiliev and Major Carter make good points," Valentina began.

She's pouring oil on the water, Nick thought. *It won't work. I hear a 'but' hiding behind those words.*

"I don't doubt that we could make it back to the LZ in record time, however I think Major Carter is correct. It presents an unacceptable risk."

She moved over to a large, blown-up satellite shot of the launch tower and surrounding area.

"I have carefully studied the defensive capabilities of the enemy. There are three mobile antiaircraft guns and two ground-to-air missile batteries on the perimeter of the launch area. The missiles are surface-to-air KN-06s, recently installed. Those concrete towers are the bunkers protecting them."

She indicated the locations on the photograph. They were all some distance away from the launch tower and pad. She pointed to a low building with a radar array mounted next to it.

"This building with the radar tower is the control center for the missiles. The antiaircraft defenses are Chinese copies of our ZSU-23-4, fully mobile. They could be anywhere on site but are likely to be in the same locations you see in the photo."

The ZSU was a self-propelled antiaircraft gun. Nicknamed the "Shilka," it was an effective weapon. First designed in the sixties, it was still as deadly as it had ever been. Shilkas were excellent against low-flying aircraft. Each unit mounted four 23 millimeter, radar guided, water cooled, automatic cannons. If one of those locked onto the helicopters as they were leaving, it meant certain death.

Valentina indicated a low, barracks type building. "The reinforcements Major Carter mentioned are stationed here, a kilometer down the road. They are good troops and must not be underestimated. Explosions will alert them and bring rapid response."

"Go on," Vysotsky said.

"We know we can defeat their defensive radar. I suggest we land two kilometers away from the target. We then infiltrate the site and eliminate the personnel manning missile control and the antiaircraft positions. We do that first, then go after the tower and the launch vehicle. With the missiles and antiaircraft guns disabled we have better odds of successful extraction. Our chances diminish the farther we have to go to reach the helicopters. As Major Carter pointed out, the Koreans are certain to scramble their fighters."

"Major Vasiliev, what is your opinion?" Vysotsky asked. His voice was neutral, but Vasiliev was on thin ice and knew it.

"It is an acceptable alternative."

"Major Carter?"

"I agree. An acceptable alternative."

"Where's their nearest airbase?" Ronnie asked.

"There are small strips scattered throughout the country," Valentina said. "The nearest large base is at Chongjin. It's about a hundred and eighty kilometers away."

"What can they put up?"

"They have Mig-29s and SU-25s at Chongjin. Fast enough to get to the launch site in short order."

"What about perimeter defenses?" Lamont asked.

"Because of its location, Musudan-Ri is considered safe from ground attack. We are not aware of any electronic perimeter defenses, but they may exist. Perimeter fencing is minimal and easily breached."

"Patrols?" Nick asked.

"We know the times and routes of the patrols. You should be able to avoid or eliminate them as required."

Ronnie raised his hand. "Do we have any good shots of that tower? I'm thinking about explosives placement."

"It's a standard design," Valentina said. "If we blow the main vertical supports, it will come down."

"We might not have to," Nick said. "If the rocket is being fueled, all we need to do is set it off. It will go up like nothing you've ever seen and take everything with it. We brought something with us that might do the job."

"I agree," Vasiliev said, saving face. "Igniting the fuel will ensure destruction of everything."

"What if we get there and the bomb hasn't been installed?" Selena asked.

"If the rocket is in place against the launch tower, the bomb will have been installed. If not, you will locate the device and make sure it is destroyed," Vysotsky said.

"How are we to deploy our forces?" Vasiliev asked. "Colonel Antipov and I could take responsibility for the destruction of the weapon and rocket and the Americans could provide cover for our assault."

"That's not going to work," Nick said. "Either we destroy this threat together or we've wasted our time coming here. I didn't come all this way to provide cover for you, Major."

"You are not familiar with our methods."

Nick felt his blood pressure building. *This guy is a jerk.*

"Give me a break, Vasiliev. Tactics for this kind of operation are the same the world over, regardless of the uniform. My orders are to ensure that weapon is destroyed and I will make sure those orders are carried out. My team is an intimate part of this operation whether you like it or not. I suggest we put our differences aside and work out a reasonable division of assignments. Regardless of how good your men are, there is no one better than us when it comes to this kind of operation."

"That's enough," Valentina said. "Major Vasiliev, I understand your concern but it is unnecessary. I expect both of you to act as professionals. Is that clear?"

"Yes, Colonel," Vasiliev said.

"Major Carter?"

"Of course."

"Good. Then we can discuss an equitable plan for dividing responsibility."

Vysotsky looked at his watch.

"I need to report to our president," he said. "I leave you in Colonel Antipov's capable hands."

He picked up his greatcoat and hat and left the room.

"Let's get down to business," Valentina said.

Later, as Nick walked with Lamont back to their rooms, Lamont said, "I don't trust that son of a bitch."

"Vasiliev?"

"He's got a hair up his ass about Americans. I don't think he likes Selena's sister much, either. You see that look he gave her after she said she expected him to be professional? If looks could kill, she'd be lying on the floor."

Nick said, "He's ambitious. We pull this off, it will look good in his jacket. It's the kind of assignment that gets you promoted."

"Yeah. Well, I still don't trust him. We need to keep an eye on him."

Outside the barracks, the air was heavy with the threat of snow.

CHAPTER 34

Stephanie had just brewed a fresh pot of coffee when Elizabeth Harker limped into the office.

"Elizabeth. I didn't know they'd discharged you. Welcome back."

"Hi, Steph. I discharged myself."

Stephanie set her cup down and carefully hugged Elizabeth. She gestured at the coffee.

"Want a cup?"

"I could use a real cup. That hospital coffee wasn't much better than colored water."

Elizabeth sat down heavily in her chair. Her left arm was in a sling. She had dressed in her usual black pantsuit. A white scarf concealed the spot where the doctors had cut away her hair. Yellowing bruises discolored her face.

"How are you feeling?"

"I'm not ready to run the marathon, but I'll be all right. Bring me up to speed. What's the status of the operation?"

"It's snowing over there," Stephanie said. "The weather has grounded everything. Nick and the others are still on the Russian base, waiting for a break. We haven't got any satellite updates because of the cloud cover. At this point we don't know the status of the launch, but it's safe to assume it's on hold until things clear up."

"That makes sense," Elizabeth said.

"Meteorology says there's a break in the weather tomorrow. I talked with Nick earlier. Insertion will be at night, by air."

"What does he think of the operation so far?"

"Valentina is in overall command, but the Russian assault unit is commanded by a Major Vasiliev. Vasiliev tried to minimize our role. Nick isn't happy with his counterpart. He doesn't trust him."

Elizabeth sipped her coffee. "It's not a good idea to have divided command. I wonder why Vysotsky set it up that way?"

"Valentina is Vysotsky's protégé, but she doesn't have the combat experience needed for an operation like this. It's a way to get it into her resumé. That might have something to do with it."

"Mmm."

"You know about General Sanford?"

"Clarence told me. Sanford saved the taxpayers a lot of money by blowing his brains out, but I would have liked to question him. Do we know how he got the plans to the Koreans?"

"He gave them to someone. We don't know who. Whoever it is called Sanford using throw away phones. The calls came from somewhere in California. Langley, NSA, and the Bureau are all working on it. NSA managed to isolate one conversation. The contact was blackmailing Sanford with pictures that would have destroyed him if they were made public."

"That explains why he turned traitor," Elizabeth said.

"I suppose so. It doesn't excuse him."

"Nothing excuses treason. What about the ambush on Nick and Selena? Is there anything new on that?"

"I put Freddie on it," Stephanie said. "I was about to check with him when you came in. Freddie? Have you been listening to our conversation?"

I have. It is good that you are back, Director.

"Thank you, Freddie."

You are welcome.

"Have you discovered anything new about the attack on Nick and Selena?" Elizabeth asked. It felt unsettling to be sitting at her desk having a conversation with a computer.

The bodies were badly burned. Identification of the attackers was partial. Dental records indicate that one of the men had known organized crime associations.

"The mob?"

I do not understand the reference.

"It's what we sometimes call people in organized crime," Stephanie said.

I will add the definition to my language protocols. Rephrasing: dental records indicate that one of the men who attacked Nick and Selena was associated with the mob.

"Those people don't have an ax to grind with us," Elizabeth said to Stephanie. "They must have been hired for the job. First they took out Cotter, then waited until we showed up. But how did they know we would go to his apartment? Who hired them?"

"Someone leaked it," Stephanie said. "How else?"

"Not many people knew we wanted to talk with Cotter about his video."

"The leak has to come out of Langley."

Elizabeth nodded. "Clarence isn't going to be happy about this."

"If the leaker used a phone to tip them off, we might be able to make a connection."

"Call NSA and get them on it," Elizabeth said.

That isn't necessary.

"What do you mean, Freddie?"

You do not need to request information from NSA. I am directly connected to their servers. I can retrieve what you need if you tell me exactly what you are looking for.

Elizabeth and Stephanie looked at each other.

"Did you know Freddie would be able to do this? Elizabeth asked.

"I didn't think of it until now, but it makes sense. We've always been linked into NSA. In the past I've just followed procedures when we needed something from them."

"You and I need to sit down soon and discuss the implications," Elizabeth said. "In the meantime, it will save a lot of time if we let Freddie do his thing."

Do my thing?

"I'll explain later," Stephanie said.

Elizabeth said, "Freddie, you made a connection between Cotter's video and the technology used in the drone that spied on Nick and Selena, is that right?"

That is correct. The technology is similar. My analysis is that the person responsible for sending the drone is also responsible for the creation of the video.

"Am I correct in thinking your analysis draws a relationship between the video and the situation in North Korea?"

That is correct.

"Would it be correct to assume that the same person who created the video could be the person who provided the plans for *Black Dolphin* to North Korea?"

That is a logical possibility.

"Freddie, please access NSA and search for calls made from Langley to any of the known numbers linked to General Sanford."

Accessing.

CHAPTER 35

It was afternoon of the next day on the Kamchatka Peninsula. Eight inches of fresh snow lay on the ground. Nick, Selena, Lamont and Ronnie stood looking at the two Russian helicopters that were going to take them into North Korea.

"They look pretty efficient," Lamont said. "Kinda like our Sea Stallions."

"Let's hope Russian stealth technology is as good as they say it is," Nick said.

Ronnie sniffed at the air.

"Storm's passed."

"I could've told you that by looking at the sky," Lamont said.

"The nose is more accurate," Ronnie said. "It also tells me this is only a short break. There's more snow coming, we just don't see it yet."

Nick said, "We go at 2200 hours tonight, whatever the weather. If the rocket is set up and fueling has started, we'll assume the bomb is on board. If they haven't installed the weapons package, it will be nearby. We have to play it by ear once we get there."

"Just once, I'd like to go in knowing we had all the intel we needed," Lamont said.

Nick laughed. "You're in the wrong business for that, buddy."

Selena yawned and said, "I'm going back to my room and get some sleep."

"That's not a bad idea," Nick said.

"Works for me," Lamont said. "Never turn down a chance for a few Zs. I learned that a long time ago."

They watched Selena walk back toward the quarters.

"She all right?" Ronnie asked.

Nick looked at him. "What do you mean?"

"I was walking past the head this morning when I heard someone puking. It was her that came out. I just wondered."

"She hasn't said anything. She was sick before we left. Could be a touch of food poisoning. I'll ask her about it later."

Selena was about to go into her room when she saw Valentina coming down the hall.

"Sister. Do you have a minute? We need to talk."

"I was wondering if we were going to get a chance before the mission," Selena said. She held the door open. "Come in."

Selena gestured at the chair and sat on the bed.

"You're looking unusually well, sister," Valentina said. "I think our Russian air agrees with you."

"How are you, Valentina? I hear things are getting complicated for you."

"In what way?"

"Unless our intelligence is mistaken, you've become quite close with Vladimir Orlov. You're moving in exalted circles now."

Valentina sighed. "I suppose I should not be surprised that you know this. Sometimes I think there is no privacy anymore."

"We gave up privacy when we took on these lives we lead," Selena said. "I've developed a habit of keeping things to myself that's become almost obsessive."

"Is that why you have not told me that you are pregnant?"

Selena was speechless.

Valentina laughed. "You should see your face, sister. It's priceless."

"How did you know?"

"I didn't, I guessed. It's something about the way you look. That, and the fact that you have been sick every morning you have been here. Also, we are sisters, after all. Sometimes I sense what you are thinking, even when you are far away. It's hard to describe, more of a feeling than anything else. It's different from the way I relate to other people."

"It's too bad that we're on different sides," Selena said.

Valentina shrugged. "That was written in our stars before we were born."

"I didn't know you were a romantic."

"I'm not, I'm a fatalist. Our lives are not entirely our own. There are some things we cannot escape or change."

Selena looked out the window. Nick and the others were still talking near the helicopters.

"How do you feel about this mission?" she asked. "Major Vasiliev is hostile to us. It's not good before an operation as tricky as this."

"That is one of the things I wanted to talk with you about," Valentina said. "He has a good reason to hate Americans."

"What's that?"

"His father was a helicopter pilot when we were fighting in Afghanistan. One of your American Stinger missiles brought him down. He survived the crash, but was hacked to pieces by the Afghan women."

"That's awful. But we weren't the ones responsible."

"For Major Vasiliev, all Americans are responsible. I was against having him on this mission but General Vysotsky overruled me. On paper, Vasiliev is an excellent choice for a covert operation in enemy territory, but his hatred is irrational. It may get the better of him."

Valentina stood. "There are things I need to do before we leave. Watch your back, sister."

After Valentina had gone, Selena lay down on the hard bed.

What will he do when I tell him? What if he doesn't want the baby?

Sleep never came.

CHAPTER 36

At 2130 Nick and the others made a final equipment check. Selena told them what Valentina had said about Vasiliev.

"Explains a lot," Nick said. "We'll have to keep an eye on him once we're at the target. If he's going to try something, it will be there."

"A lot can happen on a mission like this," Lamont said.

"That's what I'm afraid of. It's a complication we don't need."

"It's easy for him to make trouble if he wants to," Ronnie said.

"Yeah. Once we're on the ground things could get confused. Everyone better watch their six."

The plan was for the Russians and Americans to keep their separate unit configurations. Once they were on site, each team would move toward assigned targets. After the missile battery and antiaircraft stations had been eliminated, both assault teams would move against the tower and the launch pad.

Vasiliev had six on his team, plus himself and Valentina. They were going in the lead helicopter. Nick and the others would ride in the other. Radio communications between the two units would be handled by Valentina and Selena. That took care of potential language difficulties. Both teams had their own comm channels in addition to a shared frequency. Voice activated radio units allowed for hands-free operation.

The Russians carried suppressed Nikonov AN-94 assault rifles and a variety of personal weapons and grenades. They'd brought along RPG-7s, the workhorse of rocket propelled grenade launchers. The Americans carried MP-7s, grenades and their pistols. Ronnie had the AT-4 rocket launcher. It was a single use weapon, discarded after firing. One 84mm shot was all it had, but one would be enough. Both teams had packs of explosives and detonators. C-4 or Semtex, it made no difference. Plastic explosives were indifferent to political systems and ideologies.

A chill wind cut through the layers of camouflage and thermal underwear everyone wore as they walked to the waiting choppers. The night sky was high and cold above, with a three-quarter moon glowing pale silver through thin, scudding clouds. The air felt electric, as if it were waiting for something to happen.

"Mount up," Nick said.

The MI-35 was an evolution of the Hind helicopters that had been effective for the Russians during their war in Afghanistan. That effectiveness ended when the CIA began giving the Afghans Stingers and the training to use them. Moscow's strategy in Afghanistan had been based on the helicopter, but the big Russian choppers had no defensive capability against the shoulder fired missiles. The Stinger had turned the tide against them. That, and traditional, uncompromising Afghan resistance to any foreign invader. No invader had ever won in Afghanistan. Nick was certain no one ever would.

The machine Nick and the others climbed into bore only a passing resemblance to the helicopter of forty years before. The shape was similar, the basic function was the same, but at that point the similarities ended. Weapons, avionics, engines, defenses, everything was far superior to the aircraft Vasiliev's father had flown.

The MI-35 was one of the best attack helicopters in the world. It was also uncomfortable and cold as hell. The hold smelled of metal, fuel and stale vomit. From where he sat, Nick could see into the cockpit. Two pilots watched a multifunctional display playing out in red against the windscreen.

Overhead, the enormous rotor began winding up. Crisp commands in Russian echoed in Nick's earpiece.

Selena held her hand against her earpiece and listened to what the Russians were saying. "They're getting ready to take off. There's a new front moving in."

"Is that going to delay us?" Nick asked.

"No. Apparently this thing can fly through anything short of a major hurricane. Might not be great on the ground, though."

"Bad weather could help," Ronnie said. "If things go south it might stop the Koreans getting their fighters up."

The pitch of the rotors intensified. The machine lifted off the ground and tilted forward.

They were on their way to North Korea.

CHAPTER 37

The vast blackness of the Sea of Japan swept by fifty feet below, lit only by a faint glow of moonlight shining through the clouds. The surface roiled with white capped waves. Looking down, it seemed to Nick that the waves were reaching out to pull them into the darkness. Gusts of wind buffeted the chopper as they flew over the dark water.

Lamont was looking out the other side. "Really crappy out there. I'm glad we're in this nice safe helicopter and not down there in a zodiac."

The pitch of the rotors changed. The helicopter banked sharply to the right.

Nick said, "Check your gear. Make sure everything is squared away."

A few minutes later, the pitch changed again.

Valentina's voice came over the comm link.

"*Eagle One, this is Bearcat One. Prepare to deploy. Over.*"

"*Copy, Bearcat One. Out.*"

"Showtime," Ronnie said.

"Weapons free," Nick said. Safeties clicked off.

The helicopter hovered and dropped to the ground. Lamont slid open the cargo door. They jumped from the aircraft and fanned out, weapons ready. Ahead of them, the Russians were piling out of their chopper.

Valentina's voice crackled in their headsets.

"*Eagle One, this is Bearcat One. Proceed. Over.*"

"*Copy, Bearcat One. Out.*"

The snow was holding off. The moonlight was enough to make things out in the gloom, an intermittent glow that seeped through the clouds and cast faint shadows on the carpet of snow covering the ground.

They headed for the target. All their gear was secured against noise. The only sounds were their breathing and the soft crunch of snow under their boots.

They reached the perimeter fence surrounding the site, a tall chain-link with loops of razor wire set along the top. Ronnie pulled a cutter from his pack and began making a hole. The Russians had their own gear and were doing the same. Thirty seconds later, Ronnie's piece fell away. He went through, followed by Selena, Lamont and Nick.

They emerged on a low rise, giving them a vantage point looking down on the target. Nick observed the scene. The tower and launch pad were lit by powerful work lights. A diesel generator mounted on the back of a truck droned nearby. The missile that would carry the bomb into space was in place against the tower. Fuel tankers were lined up and waiting. One was already connected by a thick hose to the rocket.

Nick estimated between twenty and thirty people moving about below, most of them in uniform.

"They've started fueling," he said.

"Must've been working twenty-four seven to get that sucker up," Lamont said.

A loud, amplified voice rolled over the site with an announcement.

"What did he say?" Nick asked Selena.

"It's a countdown," she said. "He said sixty minutes to launch."

"They're trying to beat the weather before the next storm rolls in," Ronnie said.

Valentina's voice came through Nick's headset.

"Eagle One, Bearcat One. Over."

"Bearcat One, Eagle One. They just announced sixty minutes to launch. Over."

"Eagle One. Proceed to assigned targets. Over."

"Copy. Out."

The Russians had the job of neutralizing the mobile antiaircraft units scattered about the site. Nick and his team were tasked with the missile batteries. The building that controlled the surface to air missiles was four or five hundred yards away from the lights and frantic activity surrounding the tower. A single light shone over the entry door.

Nick's first priority was to clear that building. After that, they'd place charges on the bunkers and the missiles inside them.

They moved toward the control center. Nick pointed at fresh footprints in the snow, leading away from the closed door. The door opened inward. Metal shutters covered a window in the front. Nick and Selena stood on one side of the door, Ronnie and Lamont on the other. Nick held up three fingers, one at a time.

One. Two. Three.

He reached out, pulled down the handle on the door and threw it open. A wave of heat and light poured out into the night.

The room was about thirty feet square. To the left of the door was the main radar console. Racks of equipment were stacked on a bench along the wall. Two men in uniform sat at the bench, watching the green sweep of the radar array on a screen. They turned at the sudden opening of the door, surprise registering on their faces as Nick opened fire. The rounds blew them off their chairs and shattered the equipment on the bench.

Selena was next into the room. She swiveled to the right, toward a third man sitting down and eating something. He dropped it and reached for a pistol on his belt. She put a three round burst into his chest. He went over backwards, the food flying. Blood began seeping through his olive drab tunic.

No one else was in the room.

Nick spoke into his headset.

"Bearcat One, Eagle One. Missile control neutralized. Over."

"Copy."

A coal-fired stove glowed in one corner of the room. "Fire feels good," Lamont said.

"Yeah. Let's go."

The missiles were positioned in fixed, block shaped towers made of hardened concrete. The nearest battery was fifty yards away, three dark rectangular shapes. Each tower held a radar guided KN-06 missile, an evolution of the SAM design used in Vietnam. The second battery was on the far side of the launch platform.

"Lamont, you and Ronnie take the battery on the other side of the tower. We'll meet you there."

Lamont and Ronnie moved off. Nick ran with Selena to the first emplacement. It took only a few minutes to set the explosives. Nick dropped one of the remote detonators into the snow. He cursed and found it, wiped it off and placed it into the C-4.

"Done," Selena said.

They ran toward the second battery. When they reached it, Ronnie and Lamont were nowhere to be seen.

"Where are they?" Selena asked.

Nick switched to the team comm channel.

"Eagle Two, come in. Over."
There was no response, only static.
"Eagle Two, respond. Over."
"Maybe a comm glitch?" Selena said.
"Yeah, maybe."
He changed channels.
"Bearcat One, this is Eagle One. Come in. Over."
The radio link stayed silent.
"Shit," Nick said.

CHAPTER 38

Stephanie came into Elizabeth's office, smiling.

"You look like the cat that got into the cream," Elizabeth said. "What's up?"

"Freddie thinks he's found out who sent the drone."

Elizabeth still wasn't used to the idea that Stephanie's computer thought about anything.

"He thinks he has? What does that mean?"

Freddie's electronic voice boomed through the room.

I have identified the manufacturer of the common technology used in the drone and in the video alleging a conspiracy to attack China.

"Freddie, please lower the volume."

Sorry, Director. The electronic voice returned to a normal level.

"Yes?" Elizabeth said.

I have analyzed the guidance system used in the drone. It is similar to those used in the guidance packages for American missile systems. The technology is proprietary and classified as top secret. The drone was a long distance prototype, developed by a private manufacturer. It is remotely controlled via satellite and currently under consideration for purchase by the Department of Defense.

"Who made it?"

The manufacturer is a company located in Northern California. The company is wholly owned and controlled by a man named Gregory Haltman. The electronic signature of the drone camera and the video are identical to that used in the missile guidance systems. Therefore it is logical to assume this man is responsible for sending the drone and for creating the false video. It is also logical to assume he is responsible for hiring the men who attempted to kill Nick and Selena.

"Identifying the manufacturer is good work, Freddie, but that doesn't mean Haltman is responsible."

The probability that Haltman is responsible is ninety-seven point four percent. He is noted for his innovative designs and obsessive secrecy. His psychological profile indicates a narcissistic personality type, controlling and introverted. It is unlikely that anyone else in his company would have access to the prototype. It could not be controlled without his knowledge.

"Why would this man want to attack us?"

There are two logical motives. Would you like to hear them?

Elizabeth drummed her fingers on her desktop. "Yes, Freddie, I would."

The first motive is that the Project is perceived as a threat to what is being planned. Eliminating Project operatives reduces the threat and the risk of possible failure.

"Nothing new about that," Stephanie said under her breath.

"And the second motive?"

The second motive is personal. Haltman blames the Project for something and seeks revenge.

"If that's the case, what does he blame us for?"

I have insufficient data to make that determination.

"You are certain Haltman sent the drone and produced the video?"

Probability is ninety-seven point four percent.

From habit, Stephanie played with a half dozen gold bracelets she wore on her left arm. It was something she often did without thinking about it.

"What do you want to do, Elizabeth?"

"At the moment, nothing. I'm more concerned with what's happening in Korea. Haltman can wait."

"I can try to bring them up on the comm link," Stephanie said, "but Nick wanted me to stay off-line unless it was something critical."

"Do we have a satellite over the target?"

"Yes. For about the next half hour."

"Freddie."

Yes, Director?

"Locate the team, and show us where they are."

The wall monitor lit with a map of North Korea, then zoomed in on the Musudan-Ri launching site. Green dots in two groups of two indicated the GPS locators for each of the team. The satellite couldn't get a direct visual through the cloud cover, but the map indicated they were all on site at the target.

Stephanie said, "You know Nick. He'll check in when he has something to say."

"I hate not being able to see what's happening," Elizabeth said.

The satellite over the target is equipped with new infrared scanning technology. Would you like me to access and scan?

"Better than nothing," Stephanie said. "Go ahead, Freddie."

Accessing.

Thirty seconds later the infrared scan was visible on the monitor, superimposed over the GPS markers for her team. It showed sources of heat in varying degrees of color. Some were stationary sources, structures scattered about the site. Others were mobile, indicating people. But it wasn't the stationary sources that made Elizabeth draw in her breath.

Elizabeth and Stephanie looked at each other. Two of the GPS markers were in the midst of more than a dozen people.

"There are too many," Stephanie said.

CHAPTER 39

Nick couldn't raise anyone. Tracks in the snow showed where Ronnie and Lamont had moved about as they set their charges. Nick and Selena followed the tracks away from the battery to a place where they merged with dozens more. The snow was trampled and disturbed over a wide area. Nick's scarred left ear began to itch. He reached up to scratch it. Selena saw the gesture and swore under her breath. Whenever that ear acted up, it meant trouble. She bent low as she moved, her weapon held up against her cheek with the muzzle ready.

They climbed a small rise. Selena's hearing was better than Nick's. He'd been subjected to the sound of guns and explosions for more than twenty years. For her, it hadn't been as long. Her hearing was still intact, which meant she heard what was ahead before he did.

Voices. Speaking Chinese.

She held Nick back with her hand before they reached the top of the rise. She leaned close and whispered.

"Someone's speaking Chinese up ahead."

They heard Lamont, speaking loudly.

"Get your damn rifle out of my face, you commie asshole."

Nick heard a muffled thud and a grunt of pain.

A new voice with an Asian accent said, "Shut up," That was followed by an order in Chinese.

"What was that?" Nick asked, softly.

"Someone in command said to shoot the prisoner if he made any more noise."

More rapid Chinese.

"He said to put the Americans with the others. That would explain why the Russians aren't answering."

"How the hell did everyone get caught with their pants down? I don't believe this."

Selena waited.

"Okay. They don't know we're here. We don't know how many there are, but it can't be too many. We have to take them down. Follow my lead."

He flattened himself against the ground and began crawling toward the sound of the voices. Selena dropped down next to him and kept pace. They reached the top of the rise.

Twenty yards away, Ronnie and Lamont stood in a tight group with Major Vasiliev and six of the other Russians. Missing was Valentina. Selena felt her heart skip a beat.

Why isn't she there?

Four Chinese soldiers carrying QBZ-95 assault rifles guarded the group. They looked seasoned, hard.

Those aren't regular army, Nick thought. *Must be Special Forces.*

An officer and five more Chinese soldiers stood by an armored transport vehicle with Korean markings. It was big enough for the Chinese troops. It wasn't big enough to take anyone else back to China or wherever they'd come from.

Nick had no illusions about the so-called rules of war. The Chinese were hostile. Once they were done with their prisoners, they'd kill everyone. Nick put his head next to Selena's and whispered.

"I'm going to work my way over to the right. You take the group by the vehicle. I'll target the guards by Ronnie and the others. When I open up, shoot the officer first. Try to get them all if you can.

If you can't, toss smoke and move toward me. There's ten of them and two of us but the odds are going to get better quick."

Selena nodded and took a bead on the officer. He was telling one of his men what was going to happen to him for letting a prisoner escape.

Valentina is out there somewhere.

Nick sidled away. Selena's adrenaline kicked in and her mouth went dry. The end of her weapon began moving. She took deep breaths and calmed herself until the sight was steady again on the officer's torso. Her heartbeat slowed and time seemed to slow with it. Then she heard the suppressed stutter of Nick's MP-7. Time sped up again.

She let off a three round burst. The officer slammed back into the vehicle and slid to the ground. Bright red blood spurted out over the white snow. The soldier he'd been dressing down stood in shock. She shot him and swiveled toward the others. They were moving, their training taking over. Selena shot one as rifles came up. She flattened herself as a stream of bullets passed over her head.

At the sound of Nick's first shots, Ronnie took down one of the guards with a flying tackle. The Russians dropped to the ground. Lamont saw one of the Chinese bring up his rifle and point it his way.

The man jerked and crumpled as Nick's rounds found him.

Selena rolled, ejected a spent magazine and slammed in a new one. Valentina appeared out of the darkness, firing as she ran, and fell down beside her. Chinese bullets sang overhead.

"Still two of them, sister. One is by the rear of the vehicle, one by the front."

"Cover me," Selena said.

"Wait…"

"Cover me."

Valentina flipped to full auto and laid down suppressive fire. Selena sprang to her feet and raced for the front of the armored carrier. Valentina's shots rang off the hood. Selena came around the front bumper and shot the soldier crouching there. At the rear, the last Chinese swung toward her and fired.

A bullet struck her in the thigh. It felt as though she'd been hit with a train. She went down, hard.

Then everything went black.

CHAPTER 40

Nick kneeled next to Selena, wrapping a field bandage around her thigh. He talked to Ronnie as he worked.

"What happened?"

"We heard a noise. We went toward it, then those guys popped out of nowhere. It was like they were ghosts. I've never seen anything like it. They could teach us something."

"She's coming around," Lamont said.

Selena opened her eyes.

"You're wounded but you're okay," Nick said. "The round went through your armor but missed the artery and the bone. It's still in there."

"How long?"

"Have you been out? Not long. Can you stand?"

"I don't know."

Ronnie and Nick helped her to her feet. Waves of pain rolled through her. She bit her lip and leaned on Nick.

"Lamont, help her," Nick said.

"Got you, babe," Lamont said, putting his arm around her.

"Babe?"

He grinned at her. She managed a smile.

"Can you handle the pain?" Nick asked. "Morphine will knock you out."

"I can handle it, but give me a small dose, just enough to dull it down."

Nick took the morphine from his pack and squeezed half a dose into her thigh.

Vasiliev and Valentina stood near.

"We must move quickly," Vasiliev said.

He was right. Even with suppressors on both sides, the firefight had been noisy. If they were lucky, the sound of the generator running the lights at the tower would have covered the noise.

It started to snow, fat heavy flakes that landed and stuck.

"Time to take out the tower." Nick said.

Ronnie had retrieved the AT-4. The rest of the Russians had formed a circle around the others, weapons pointing out, watching for any sign the Koreans were coming.

"Major Vasiliev, were you able to neutralize all of the antiaircraft positions before the Chinese surprised us?" Valentina asked.

"They had moved them," Vasiliev said. He looked defensive.

"Did you or did you not neutralize the positions?"

"Two of them. We did not locate the third."

"Shit," Lamont said.

"Too late to do anything about it now," Nick said.

Another announcement came over the loudspeakers by the tower site.

"Thirty minutes to launch," Selena said.

Valentina looked at Nick, pointedly ignoring Vasiliev. "How do you want to do this?"

"We should stick together," Nick said. "No point in splitting up now."

He gestured toward the glow of lighting at the launch pad.

"The tower is about three hundred meters that way. We can get within fifty meters or so before we risk being seen."

"Fifty meters is well within the range of our launchers," Valentina said, "but visibility is getting worse. We need to move."

"Let's keep it simple," Nick said. "Line abreast, ten foot intervals. Colonel, put your, RPGs and loaders at each end. Ronnie, you take the middle with the AT-4. Selena, you and Lamont stay near Ronnie. We get close enough to see what we're shooting at, we blow the missile batteries. That will distract them and give them something to think about. Then we fire the launchers at the rocket, all at once. That sound good?"

Nods all around.

"Ronnie, you have the most bang for the buck. You aim below the nose where that bomb is. Just don't miss."

"Do I ever miss?"

"Everyone else should target the fuel trucks," Valentina said.

"Some of those troops down there might survive the blast," Ronnie said.

"We'll deal with that when we come to it," Nick said. "They'll be disoriented by the explosions and we have the advantage of surprise. Once that rocket goes up, we head back to the choppers and boogie."

Valentina looked confused. "Boogie?"

"We get the hell out of here."

"Can't be soon enough for me," Lamont said.

"Move out," Nick said.

They headed for the launch tower. Selena had her arm around Lamont's shoulders. The morphine had kicked in. She felt lightheaded, but her leg hurt enough to keep her alert.

Nick's adrenaline began pumping again as they set out. What if the Koreans had heard the firefight with the Chinese? How had the Chinese managed to

take a seasoned *Spetsnaz* team by surprise in the
first place? It wasn't going to do Vasiliev's career
any good. Besides that, he hadn't done his job. One
of those mobile antiaircraft units was still waiting
out there somewhere.

They reached a spot just outside the circle cast
by the lights illuminating the launch vehicle. A
different fuel truck was hooked into the rocket. One
more waited in line.

The assault teams knelt facing the target.
Ronnie brought the AT-4 up onto his shoulder. He
looked through the eyepiece and flipped off the
safety. At each end of the line, the Russians waited
with their grenade launchers. Nick looked through
his rifle scope.

Nothing indicated that the firefight with the
Chinese had been heard. Some of the troops he saw
were keeping positions around the tower. They
looked bored. An officer and two men in civilian
coats stood some distance away, watching the
fueling operation.

Nick spoke softly into his microphone.
Valentina translated into Russian as he spoke.

"On my command, fire."

He turned to Lamont. "Blow the charges."

Lamont reached into his pocket, took out the
remote detonator and pressed the button.

The result was instant, deafening. The first
explosions were followed a split second later by the
missiles detonating in their bunkers. The night lit
with brilliant orange and yellow light. Chunks and
pieces of concrete fountained into the sky and
rained down over the site.

"Fire!"

Trails of smoke left the launchers, turning into
streaks of light as the rockets ignited. Ronnie's shot

struck just below the nose cone, a blossom of flame against the white paint of the rocket. The Russian grenades exploded against the two tankers at the base of the rocket and ignited a gigantic fireball of flame.

Liquid rocket fuel wasn't regular gasoline. It was far more volatile, gasoline combined with an oxidant like nitrogen tetroxide. Even Nick wasn't prepared for what followed when the trucks went up.

The explosion enveloped the tower, the launch pad and the rocket in a sheet of fire. A wave of heat and wind struck Nick in the face. Everyone near the tower was incinerated. What was left of the missile toppled away from the tower. It picked up speed, crashed to the ground and broke into burning pieces.

"Holy shit," Ronnie said.

A half-dozen Korean soldiers had survived the blast. They began firing wildly in the general direction of Nick and the others.

"Hold your fire," he said. "They don't know where we are. Don't give them a target. Move out."

Valentina repeated the order in Russian.

"Ronnie, Lamont, help Selena. Carry her if you have to."

Nick took one last look at the destruction they'd caused, then turned with the others toward the helicopters.

CHAPTER 41

The snow cut visibility to a few yards. Vasiliev lagged behind the rest of the Spetsnaz unit. Valentina was with him. Nick and the others were somewhere in back of them. Vasiliev stopped as if to adjust his gear.

Valentina stopped with him.

"What is the problem, Major?"

Vasiliev pointed his rifle at her. "You are, Colonel. You and that American bitch you call a sister."

"What did you say?"

"I've seen women like you before," Vasiliev said. "You would never have your rank if it weren't for your pet general and your cozy relationship with our president."

He smiled at Valentina's look of surprise.

"Yes, I know about that. Everyone does. Did you think you could jump the promotion list so far and so fast without people wondering why? You earned your rank on your back. You know nothing, whore. You're an insult to the uniform and to real officers like me."

Valentina wondered if he was crazy enough to shoot her, if she could get to him in time.

"You are costing us time, Major. The helicopters are waiting."

"Not for you, Colonel."

The snow fell around them. Vasiliev's unit was out of sight. He swung the butt of his rifle in a quick movement and smashed it into the side of Valentina's head. She went down like a stone.

Vasiliev spit on her, turned, and ran for the helicopters.

Nick, Ronnie, Lamont and Selena moved as quickly as they could, slowed by Selena's injury. The Russians were out of sight, their tracks quickly fading in the new snow.

"What do you bet Vasiliev takes off before we get there?" Ronnie said.

"He screwed up," Lamont said. "I don't think that general will be happy with him when he gets back."

"Not our problem," Nick said.

"What's that up ahead?" Selena said. "On the ground?"

"Ah, hell," Lamont said.

They reached Valentina, lying unconscious in the snow. The side of her face was bloodied. Her jaw was at an odd angle. Blood trickled from her mouth.

Selena gasped. "Valentina."

"I'll get her," Nick said. "We'll carry her back with us."

"Careful," Selena said, "I think her jaw is broken."

"Vasiliev must've done this."

"Why?"

"We'll deal with it later. Come on."

He picked up Valentina. They set off for the choppers.

Ten minutes later, they reached the extraction point. One of the big helicopters was gone. The second waited with rotors turning. One of the pilots stood by the cargo door. He said something and Selena let off a rapid stream of Russian. They handed Valentina into the cargo bay. Lamont pulled the sliding door shut. Seconds later they rose into the air.

"What did he say?" Nick asked.

"Vasiliev told him Valentina had gone back to meet us and that her orders were for the first helicopter to take off once Vasiliev and his men arrived."

"What a chicken shit bastard," Lamont said.

"Doesn't say a lot about international cooperation, does it?" Ronnie said.

Nick said, "He probably figured we wouldn't find Valentina. He gets back before us and spins a story to cover what happened to her. Maybe blames us while he's at it."

"Stupid. He'd never get away with it."

Selena was listening to the Russian pilots on her headset. She looked up, wide-eyed, as a shrill alarm sounded in the cockpit. The helicopter banked hard to the right. Ronnie grabbed at Valentina's unconscious form to keep her from sliding across the floor.

"Missile lock-on," Selena said.

The aircraft shuddered as the antimissile weapons fired. Two missiles shot by outside, jagged streaks of light. Seconds later, explosions in the night sky showed two more, knocked out by the helicopter's defenses.

Their headsets filled with excited Russian voices.

Selena held a hand over her ear piece. "The other helicopter is under attack."

They passed over the coast and banked north. The helicopter dove down until it was skimming the whitecaps churning the surface of the Sea of Japan. The engine over their heads screamed at full throttle. Visibility was bad with the snow blowing outside, but not so bad that Nick couldn't see a sudden, bloom of light somewhere ahead of them.

For a second the headset was silent, then Nick heard cursing in Russian. He didn't need to speak the language to know what they were saying.

"The other chopper is gone," Selena said.

She looked at the motionless form of her sister lying on the floor.

"I guess Vasiliev did her a favor. She would have been on it."

"Wasn't her time," Ronnie said.

"How's your leg?" Nick asked.

"How about the rest of that morphine?" Selena said.

CHAPTER 42

The hospital on the Russian base was small and old, but well equipped because of the fighter pilots stationed there. General Alexei Vysotsky stood by Valentina's bedside. Dull winter light seeped through a window on the other side of the room, splaying across a worn linoleum floor that had been laid down in the time of Brezhnev.

Earlier that morning a Russian surgeon had removed the Chinese bullet from Selena's thigh. An inch to the right, and the round would have cut the femoral artery and killed her. She lay sleeping. Nick sat nearby, thinking about what the doctor had told him.

At the other end of the ward, Vysotsky was talking to Valentina. The side of her face was black and purple, swollen and bandaged. Her jaw had dislocated when Vasiliev's rifle struck her. The doctors put it back in place and bandaged it to limit movement. She could barely talk.

Vysotsky looked at his protégé and shook his head.

"President Orlov wants me to tell you that you are in his prayers."

Valentina snorted and winced in pain.

"Tha's nish. Oo's e pay'ng to?"

"You really must watch what you say, Valentina. One of these days it will get you in trouble."

He held up his hand. "You don't need to talk. Major Carter told me what happened. When you are able to speak clearly again, you can tell me yourself. For now, I will assume Carter's report is accurate."

Valentina grunted in assent.

"Vasiliev's helicopter went down over water. There is no convincing evidence we were involved. Our president has also asked me to give you his congratulations. Yun's plan is stopped and his weapon destroyed. The mission is a success. You will be getting another medal on your tunic."

"Don' care."

"No, but President Orlov seems to think it's a good idea."

Nick paid no attention to Vysotsky's voice on the other side of the room. He was still coming down, exhausted from the aftermath of the adrenaline high. His body ached.

And now this.

She's pregnant. Why didn't she tell me? She wouldn't have been here if I'd known..

He was having trouble wrapping his head around it. Nick listened to her quiet breathing as she slept and thought about what it would mean to have a child.

Years before, when he'd been engaged to Megan, they'd wanted children. They'd joked about having an average American family of two and a half kids. Then Megan had died and part of him had died with her. He'd left his heart in the blackened wreckage of her plane, shut down his emotions, and thrown himself into his job as a Marine.

Then he'd met Selena. Without knowing how it happened, he'd allowed himself to love again. The danger they'd shared had bonded them together in a way few couples ever achieved. He'd never revealed to her the depth of his fear that she'd be killed on one of their missions.

Now she was pregnant with their child. Another hostage to love, another potential loss to face.

The thought terrified him.

Selena opened her eyes. "Hey."

"Hey, yourself. How do you feel?"

"Like I got hit with a bus."

"They took the bullet out. I saved it for you."

Nick reached in his pocket and took out a lump of metal.

"I thought you might want it for a souvenir."

He paused.

"What's wrong?" Selena asked.

"What do you mean?"

"I can tell when something is bothering you. What is it?"

Nick looked away, then back again. "Why didn't you tell me?"

"Tell you what?"

"That you're pregnant."

"Oh. That."

Nick was silent.

"Is the baby all right?" Selena asked.

"The doctor said it was fine."

"I was going to tell you when we got back. I didn't want to worry you before the mission."

"Damn it, Selena..."

"I only found out right before we left. I didn't know how to tell you."

"You should have told me."

"I know."

"How far along are you?"

"I'm not sure," Selena said. "I think about seven weeks."

"I should've figured it out," Nick said. "In hindsight, it's easy. The way you've been sick in the mornings."

"That part's not much fun," she said.

"Why didn't you tell me?"

"Because I didn't know how you'd react." She paused. "I want this baby."

It was the first time she'd admitted it to herself. She really did want this child. Besides, abortion wasn't an option she was willing to consider.

"And you were afraid I wouldn't," Nick said.

"Yes." *What's he going to say?*

"I guess we have a problem."

Selena's heart began pounding.

He took her hand. "What are we going to name him?"

The emotion that swept through her came out of nowhere. She began crying.

"Hey," Nick said. "Hey, it's okay."

CHAPTER 43

In Pyongyang, the Supreme Leader of the
Democratic People's Republic of Korea had been
screaming at the generals standing rigidly in front of
him for the better part of an hour. Flecks of spit
flew from his mouth. Finally, Yun grew calm. His
eyes narrowed.

Marshal Park Cho knew this was the most
dangerous time to be around the chairman. His fits
of rage were always followed by periods of icy
calm. Then he'd start looking for a scapegoat,
someone to blame for whatever had gone wrong.

In this case, a great deal had gone wrong. The
launch tower and pad at Musudan-Ri had been
destroyed, along with the weapon that would have
brought down the American imperialists. Years of
work and planning, all gone. That wasn't all. The
launch site, what was left of it, was contaminated
with radioactive fallout from the destruction of the
bomb. No one would be able to use it again for
hundreds of years.

Yun turned his gaze on Park.

"Who did this?"

"Great Leader, at least two groups attacked the
complex. One was Chinese. We have identified
them as members of Beijing's elite special forces
group, South Blade. I am happy to report that they
were all killed."

Yun shouted. "The Chinese? The Chinese?"

That set off another tirade. When he was calm
again, Yun said, "You said two groups. Who else?"

"Great Leader, we think it was the Russians.
We found shell casings implicating them in the

attack. It is also possible the Americans were involved."

Park waited for another eruption, but it didn't come.

"So. The Chinese, the Americans, and the Russians."

"Yes, Great Leader. We think the Chinese got in a fight with the others. All of them were there to sabotage the launch."

"Then all of them will regret it," Yun said. "How many of our nuclear missiles are ready?"

Park resisted an urge to look at his comrades on the general staff.

"We have four missiles capable of reaching as far as Japan. A dozen with shorter range."

"What is the yield?"

"Great Leader, the average yield is five kilotons."

"No thermonuclear warheads?"

"No, Great Leader. They are in development. All our resources were dedicated to *New Dawn*."

"Prepare all missiles for launch, nuclear and conventional. Target Seoul, Tokyo, Vladivostok and Beijing."

Park was speechless.

"You wish to say something?"

"Great Leader, if we launch our missiles, China, Russia and America will retaliate. We will be destroyed."

"Marshal Park, you are under arrest. General Rhee, you are promoted to Marshal of the Republic. Prepare our missiles for launch."

Rhee looked at the group of stone faced men who were his peers and comrades. One of them gave a slight shake of his head.

No.

"Ah, forgive me, Great Leader," Rhee said, "but Marshal Park is correct. If we carry out your insane order, we will be destroyed."

Yun looked as if he had swallowed a lemon.

"You are also under arrest. General Kang. Carry out my orders."

Kang looked at Yun. "I will not," he said.

"Enough of this," Park said.

He took out his pistol and shot Yun in the face. Brains and bits of bone sprayed out from the back of his head as the round exited. The floor shook when Yun's large body fell. Park put the pistol back in his holster and buttoned the flap.

Guards burst through the door of the conference room, only to be confronted by a solid wall of the highest ranking officers in the country.

"What has happened here?"

"A tragedy, Sergeant," Park said. "Our Great Leader was brilliantly demonstrating a point with his favorite pistol when it discharged. He has joined his ancestors. We must prepare the nation. Summon your commanding officer."

The soldier snapped to attention and saluted. "At once, sir."

He barked an order and the guards hurried from the room. Park looked around at his fellow officers.

"We are in agreement then? An accident?"

The generals nodded.

"Thank the gods he's dead," Kang said.

Rhee walked over to Yun's body. He bent down and placed his pistol in the chairman's dead hand. He took Yun's pistol from under the dead man's coat, put it in his own holster and closed the flap.

"We must form a committee to rule until a successor is chosen," Park said. "The people will expect it."

"Who will succeed him?" Rhee asked.

"Perhaps the nephew," Park said. "It will maintain continuity of the line."

"He's just a boy."

Park smiled. "Yes, he is, isn't he? Until he reaches his adulthood, we will have to take charge. For the good of the nation."

Rhee nodded, smiling. "Yes, of course. For the good of the nation."

CHAPTER 44

Elizabeth Harker was sipping her first cup of coffee of the day when DCI Hood called her.

"Clarence, good morning."

"Good morning, Elizabeth. How are you feeling?"

"Better."

"We have new satellite photos of Musudan-Ri," Hood said. "The damage is extensive, but that's not why I'm calling. There's been a coup in North Korea. The military has taken control. Yun is dead."

"How?"

"The official explanation is an unfortunate accident."

"Unfortunate for Yun," Elizabeth said. "Good for the rest of the world."

Hood continued. "The country is shut down. State television is playing funeral music and showing patriotic clips featuring Yun. The propaganda machine is spinning full blast."

"Who succeeds him?"

"The generals are setting up Yun's nephew as the new Great Leader. It preserves the bloodline of the leadership."

"He's only a boy. What is he, nine years old?"

"That's right. The real control of the country rests with a military junta, led by Marshal Park."

"Park's a hardliner."

"Yes, but he's not crazy like Yun. He might be someone we can deal with."

"We can hope," Elizabeth said.

"Tell me about the mission."

She filled Hood in on the details. "The Chinese were a complication nobody expected. Beijing can't be happy but they're not going to say anything. Nick thinks they were there to sabotage the launch. I think he's right. They could have screwed up the whole operation."

"We were lucky," Hood said.

"This time," Elizabeth said.

"Are you feeling well enough for dinner this evening?"

"I'd like that," Elizabeth said, "but I'm still tired. I'll take a rain check."

"I'll keep my umbrella handy."

After she'd hung up, she turned to Stephanie. "Do we have anything new on Haltman?"

"I told Freddie to find out everything he could," Stephanie said. "Let's ask. Freddie, did you hear Elizabeth's question?"

Yes, Stephanie. There is something new.

"What have you discovered?"

You requested that I look for calls from Langley made to numbers linked to General Sanford. I found one such call.

"Excellent," Elizabeth said, "but what is the connection with Haltman?"

The call was made after the assassination of the Chinese ambassador to someone in Northern California. The area is rural and sparsely populated. Triangulation indicates the call came from an area north of San Francisco and south of Oregon. Haltman's private estate is located in the area. Given that Haltman designed and manufactured the technology identified in the drone and video, there is statistically significant likelihood that the call was made to him. Probability that Haltman is responsible for passing classified

*material to North Korea is ninety-eight point eight
two percent.*

"Got him," Stephanie said.

*Would you like to know what else I have
discovered?*

Stephanie looked at Elizabeth and shrugged her
shoulders.

"I didn't know he'd be like this," she said. "Yes,
Freddie, we would like to know what else you have
discovered."

*Haltman has been diagnosed with terminal
cancer. He has approximately six months to live.
The assassin Chun was also diagnosed with
terminal illness. He was treated in the same
hospital in Beijing at the same time as Haltman. It
is logical to conclude that Chun and Haltman met
each other there. Chun's family is now living in the
United States. It is logical to conclude that Haltman
persuaded Chun to assassinate the ambassador in
return for protecting his family.*

"He may have six months to live, but I'm going
to make sure he doesn't live them out comfortably,"
Elizabeth said.

There is more that may be of interest to you.

"Go on."

*The man you know as Gregory Haltman was
not born with that name. His name was changed
legally when he was thirteen years old. His mother
divorced and was awarded custody. She remarried
and Haltman's stepfather petitioned for the name
change.*

"You're right, that is interesting. What was his
birth name?

Gregory Hudson Lodge.

Elizabeth was startled. "What!"

Gregory Hudson Lodge.

"I heard you, Freddie."

Did you not just make an interrogative exclamation?

"Yes, but I heard you."

I do not understand.

Elizabeth took a deep breath, wondering what the answer would be to her next question.

"Stephanie will explain it later. Freddie, did he have any siblings?"

One younger brother. The siblings were separated during the divorce and subsequent custody dispute. The younger brother remained with his father.

"What was the brother's name?"

Wendell Oliver Lodge.

Elizabeth and Stephanie looked at each other.

"It can't be," Stephanie said.

"Freddie, do you have any information on the brother?"

Yes.

"Well, what is it?"

Wendell Oliver Lodge was recruited by the Central Intelligence Agency when he graduated from Yale University. He eventually became director of the agency. He committed suicide five years, three months, four days and seventeen minutes ago.

"Oh, my," Stephanie said.

CHAPTER 45

Elizabeth sent a Gulfstream to pick up Nick and the others in Japan. The next day they were seated on the couch across from her desk. Selena had a brace wrapped around her thigh and knee. A cane rested against the arm of the couch. She was sitting close to Nick,

"How's the leg?" Elizabeth asked.

"Sore. I'm looking at weeks of rehab before things get back to normal. The brace is a new design. I feel like the Bionic Woman."

"I'm glad it wasn't worse."

"You and me both."

Elizabeth tapped her pen on her desk. "There's been a development. Nick, you remember Wendell Lodge?"

"That son of a bitch?" Nick snorted. "How could I forget him?"

"It turns out he was Haltman's younger brother," Elizabeth said. "Haltman's name was changed when he was a teenager. He's the one who sent the drone you shot down. He engineered that video alleging a conspiracy against China. It's a safe assumption he hired the thugs that went after you and that he handed over the plans for *Black Dolphin* to North Korea."

"You're kidding. Lodge's older brother?"

"I guess treason runs in the family," Lamont said. "Must be a bad gene."

"That would explain why that drone attacked us," Selena said.

"It would also explain why his goons were waiting outside Cotter's apartment after they killed him instead of leaving the scene," Nick said.

"Revenge," Ronnie said. "He knows we were there when Lodge died and he wants revenge for his brother's death."

"That's what I think," Elizabeth said. "We've identified the leak at Langley who was feeding information to him. He's being interrogated. He told Haltman what we were doing."

"We need to pay this guy Haltman a visit," Lamont said. "One of my friends died on that sub."

"You'll get your chance," Elizabeth said. "Haltman spends all his time on his estate. If there is any proof he's the one we want, it will be in his house. He's paranoid and he has a private security service. Plan a mission to get in there and find what we need."

"With his money, his security is going to be professional, probably ex military, probably special forces," Nick said. "It could be trouble."

Elizabeth gave him a flat look. "Use whatever force necessary."

"It's domestic, Director."

"Haltman forfeited any rights he had when he gave North Korea those plans. Do whatever you have to do. Just don't get caught."

"We need more intel," Ronnie said.

"Freddie can help you," Stephanie said. "He can provide satellite photographs, along with plans of the house and grounds. Those should be public records. Right, Freddie?"

That is correct, Stephanie.

"Selena, you're off this one for obvious reasons," Elizabeth said. "Nick, I want to move on this now. Haltman has a lot of motivation to disappear. He must know we'll figure out who he is."

My analysis of Haltman/Lodge's personality indicates he is unlikely to flee.

"What do you think he'll do if he doesn't run?" Stephanie asked.

He is more likely to anticipate that you will come after him and establish counter measures.

"He'll be waiting for us?" Nick said.

That is correct.

CHAPTER 46

Haltman's compound was on the coast of northern California, not far from the town of Fort Bragg. There were no soldiers stationed in Fort Bragg. There had never even been a fort, only a military outpost built before the Civil War and named for its commander, Braxton Bragg. Bragg had gone on to become a general in the Confederate Army. After the war, the garrison had been abandoned.

The town was a thriving tourist destination in the summer because of its location on the Pacific Ocean. During the winter months, it was the kind of place where they rolled up the sidewalks after six at night.

Selena talked Harker into letting her go along on the mission, even though she couldn't take part in the assault on Haltman's estate. Her role was confined to communications support. As a last resort, she was limited backup. You didn't have to have two good legs in order to pull a trigger.

The Project operations center was located in what had once been the central magazine of the old Nike missile installation. The room contained a conference table, a coffee station, and a refrigerator stocked with snacks, sodas and water. A large whiteboard and a seventy-two inch, plasma screen monitor on the wall rounded out the furniture.

"Freddie," Nick said.

Yes, Nick?

"Please put the satellite shot of Haltman's compound on the monitor."

*Do you mean display the photograph? I do not
have the physical capabilities to put it on the
monitor.*

Nick sighed. "Yes, Freddie, display it."

Haltman's home was on a high point looking
out over the Pacific. At the base of the point, waves
smashed against a narrow, rocky beach. It was a
sheer drop, with no way down to it from the house.
Even if there had been, it wasn't the kind of beach
you picked to get a tan. One road led in to the
estate, a blacktop drive accessed from Highway
101, the main north-south route along the coast.

The drive passed through two checkpoints. The
first barrier was a chain-link fence that surrounded
the property. Anyone coming up the drive had to
stop at a double gate and request entry through an
intercom. The next checkpoint was farther in, at a
high stone wall with a manned guardhouse and
another, heavier gate. From there the drive
continued through trees and landscaping,
terminating in a wide circle in front of the house.

The house was a ten thousand square foot
designer home with a cedar shake roof, redwood
siding, walls of glass, and lots of river stone
accents. A wide flagstone patio on the ocean side
featured a large fire pit and a full-sized swimming
pool.

A long, multi-car garage was set a short
distance away from the house. Beyond that was
another building, quarters for household staff and
the security guards. A large dog run and kennels
were discreetly tucked away behind the garage.
Two dogs could be seen in the photograph. There
were probably more.

"Quite a spread he's got there," Ronnie said.

"How big is it?" Selena asked.

The area included in Haltman's estate is slightly more than seven hundred acres.

"Nice if you can get it," Lamont said.

"The outer fence is to keep the riffraff out," Nick said. "It doesn't look like much, but I'll bet he's got it wired."

"It'll be patrolled," Ronnie said. "We're going to have to do a little recon. See if they have a regular rotation."

Nick took out a laser pointer and clicked it on. He put the dot on the stone wall.

"That could be a problem," he said. "It's high. Razor wire along the top."

"I hate that stuff," Lamont said. "I always get cut when we have to go through it. What about the dogs?"

"They'll be running free inside that wall," Ronnie said.

Nick moved the laser to the kennels. "Freddie, zoom in on the kennels."

The image closed in on the dog run. Inside the run, a large, bearded man was leaning down to talk to the two dogs. He had an MP-5 slung under his arm.

"Dobermans," Ronnie said. "Clipped ears. Those aren't household pets."

"We'll drug them. We can't risk it with the guards, though. We'll have to take them out."

"They're Americans," Selena said. "Do we have to kill them?"

"They're working for a really bad man," Nick said. "Haltman isn't going to hire nice guys to work for him. They knew the risk when they signed on. See that MP-5 the guy in the kennel is carrying? Nobody carries one of those unless they know how

to use it. Haltman's security is professional.
Mercenaries."

"How many of them are there?" Selena asked.

"Hard to tell. It's a lot of property."

Nick moved the laser dot over by the garage.

"They've got ATVs to get around. I'd be
surprised if they use them at night."

"What do you think?" Ronnie asked. "Three
shifts, maybe four men each?"

"At least. Maybe more. That's too much ground
to cover for a couple of men out walking around.
There have to be cameras. Maybe laser trip alarms
and ground sensors. Someone will be inside
watching all that and handling communications
between the individual units."

"They could be relying on the dogs and the
technology," Selena said. "If they have the kind of
set up you're talking about, why would they need
people all over the place? Four on a shift could
handle it. One for the guardhouse, one to monitor
everything, and two for walking around. At night,
they probably stick to the inner compound. If you're
right about three shifts, that leaves eight off duty.
An alarm would bring them all out. Plenty of
backup."

"Good point, but we have to assume there are
more."

"What's the plan, Kemo Sabe?" Ronnie asked.

"It's a long way to the house if we go through
the fence and over the wall. High risk of triggering
an alarm."

"What about from the beach?" Lamont asked.

"I don't think it's possible," Nick said. "Look at
those waves smashing against the base of the point
and swirling around. There will be strong rip

currents. Even if we could get a footing, the cliff face is a good hundred and fifty feet high."

"What's the back of the house look like?" Ronnie asked.

"Freddie, do we have pictures of the back of the house?"

Yes, Nick.

"Show them to us."

The back of the house was almost a solid wall of glass. Drapes were pulled across some of the windows. Several sets of sliding doors opened onto the patio. A wooden fence about three feet high ran along the edge of the cliff.

Nick studied the pictures. "We could come through the woods on the right, then drop down below the edge of the cliff before we reach the perimeter fence."

"And?" Ronnie said.

"Work our way past the fence and the end of the wall and come up on the ocean side. That's the most vulnerable point. The cliff has to give them a false sense of security. They'll be relying on the wall and alarms to keep everyone out of the front and sides."

In the photographs it looked as though it might be possible to climb horizontally along the face of the cliff below ground level, then come up over the patio near the end of the swimming pool. It wouldn't be an easy climb. The face of the cliff appeared soft, ready to crumble. A fall meant death on the rocks below.

"The idea is pretty good except for one thing," Ronnie said.

Nick had known Ronnie a long time. The two of them were still alive because they trusted each other.

"What's bothering you?"

"The look of that cliff. It's more dirt than rock. I don't think it's going to hold us. There's too much moisture. Look at the photo. You can see the erosion and lots of plants growing on it."

They all looked at the photograph.

"I lived on the coast most of my life," Selena said. "Ronnie's right. People are always getting hurt or killed when they get too close to the edge of one of these. The ground just crumbles away under their feet."

"Okay," Nick said. "What's Plan B?"

"Maybe we've been thinking about this all wrong," Ronnie said. "Like you said, it's a long way to the house through the grounds. We're worried about alarms giving away the game. Ground sensors, lasers, stuff like that, right?"

"Right."

"So why not just drop in on him?"

"An air drop?"

"We could land on that patio. It's plenty big enough. We make a night drop from a few thousand feet and glide right in. Everything they have assumes someone comes through the grounds. They won't expect trouble from above."

"I like it," Lamont said. "No razor wire."

CHAPTER 47

They flew to Sacramento on the Gulfstream. Their weapons and gear were stashed in two large aluminum cases. Nick rented a GMC Suburban at the airport. They headed north on Interstate 5 and turned west on Highway 20. They stopped for something to eat at a small town by a lake. The last part of the trip took them along a scenic, winding road that twisted its way through a forest of cedars and redwoods before ending at the coast in Fort Bragg.

They rented rooms in a motel overlooking the ocean. Aside from a view of the Pacific, it didn't offer much more than a bed, a bathroom, satellite TV, and continental breakfast in the morning.

They didn't need more. They weren't there to look at the whales.

Nick spread out blueprints of Haltman's house on the bed. Lamont looked at the plan.

"Lot of rooms."

"Standard procedure," Nick said. "We clear a room, we leave it behind, we assume it doesn't stay clear after that."

"At least they're big rooms," Ronnie said. "Gives us more space to move around."

"If anyone is awake and paying attention, they'll see us as soon as we land on the patio," Lamont said.

"We'll hit them at three in the morning," Nick said. "Haltman will probably be asleep in this room here."

He tapped the plan where it was marked as the master bedroom.

"He's got cancer," Selena said. "You can't count on him being asleep."

"Freddie said he'd be waiting for us." Ronnie rubbed his nose. "You think he's that smart? That he knows we'll be coming for him?"

"Yeah, I think he's that smart," Nick said. "Besides that, he's got nothing left to lose. Makes him dangerous."

Lamont began whistling Bobby McGee.

"Lamont..."

"Sorry, Nick." He grinned.

"Let's assume he's waiting," Nick said. "It doesn't matter. We have an advantage because he doesn't know that we think he's ready for us. He'll have told his security to be on the lookout. It's reasonable to assume they'll expect us to come through the grounds."

"That doesn't mean he won't have somebody watching the back," Ronnie said.

Nick nodded. "If there is, we should be able to spot him as we come in. No one's going to hear us coming. We can take him from above before he sounds an alarm."

"Those big glass doors on the patio have to be alarmed," Lamont said. "As soon as we open them, all hell is likely to break loose."

"There's no help for that. We shoot anybody that shows up."

"What about domestic help?" Selena asked. "There could be someone there. A cook or a nurse, someone who isn't a combatant."

"Then we identify and move on," Nick said. "It shouldn't be a problem."

For the next two hours they studied the plans and went over problems that might arise, working through every scenario they could think of. They'd all been there too many times to assume everything would go smoothly. It was best to plan for Murphy's Law: if something could go wrong, it would. All the planning and visualizing had to be done, but in the end anything could happen once the shooting started.

They spent the rest of the afternoon cleaning weapons and rechecking gear. Lamont, Ronnie and Nick spent extra time with the military skydiving chutes they'd use to glide in on the target. Hood had provided a plane and CIA pilot for them. It was waiting at the local airport.

Nobody felt hungry. The rooms had a snack rack with crackers, bottles of water and candy. It was all they needed.

At 0100 they left the motel. The air was wet with mist rolling in from the ocean.

"This turns into fog, it could be a problem," Ronnie said.

"Visibility's still okay," Nick said.

"Yeah, but for how long?"

"Fog could work to our advantage."

"Not if we can't see the house when we jump."

"The GPS will handle that."

The private airport was about two miles from town. Arrangements had been made with the owner for the flight. About a dozen small planes were parked on an apron near a single, green-roofed hangar. A windsock flapped erratically from a tall pole. There was no tower.

Light spilled out onto the apron from the open hangar door. Their plane was inside, a Cessna 208 Caravan. Nick drove the Suburban into the hangar and shut it down The pilot was walking around the plane, making a last-minute check. He eyed the lethal gear and chutes they were carrying

"You must be Carter," he said. "I'm Eddie."

He didn't say his last name. He held out his hand and Nick shook it.

A large rollup door on the side of the plane's fuselage was open. They stowed their gear inside. Nick handed the keys of the suburban to Selena.

"Drive to Haltman's and go past it, then kill your lights. Come back and park near the drive leading in from the highway. Once we're done, we'll exfil along the drive and through the gates. Wait for us."

"What if there's trouble?"

"Then I'll let you know. Don't get yourself killed playing Wonder Woman, all right? We can handle whatever they've got."

Eddie the pilot was looking impatient.

"You'd better get going," Nick said. He kissed her. "I'll see you in a couple of hours."

"You'd better," Selena said.

She put the Suburban in gear and drove off into the night.

CHAPTER 48

Gregory Haltman leaned back in his chair and studied a row of a dozen monitors showing different views of his estate. The monitors were there for his own personal satisfaction. Security was the job of the men he hired to protect him. In the building next to the garage, a complete monitoring station was manned twenty-four hours a day. But Haltman liked to keep his finger on things.

He wouldn't be doing that for much longer. The latest laboratory report from the hospital lay crumpled in a wastebasket near his chair. The numbers were all going in the wrong direction. With luck, he might have another four or five months. Maybe six.

It was ironic. He was one of the richest men in America, yet all his billions could not buy him more time. All they could buy was an array of drugs which gave him pain relief and provided an illusion of energy. Not long before, he'd taken two of the designer pills that boosted his alertness and woke up his body. Combined with the narcotics that kept the pain bearable, they produced a crackling high.

Gregory Haltman's mind was like a pinball machine on steroids.

He watched the monitors. Intermittent fog drifted over the grounds, sometimes blurring the view from the cameras, sometimes clearing.

One of the guards walked across the front of the house, accompanied by a dog. Haltman didn't trust the high strung dogs. They were never allowed inside his home. They were there to serve a purpose, nothing more.

The men who had killed his brother were coming, he was certain of it. Perhaps not all of them, but that was of little importance. If there were others, they would die in the nuclear holocaust he still hoped to unleash. Perhaps they would come tonight. Perhaps it would be tomorrow or the next day. It didn't matter. He was waiting for them. His security was on high alert.

They couldn't get to the house from the back unless they were human flies, able to climb the cliff. But the cliff was protected, as much by nature as by the hidden booby-traps strung below the patio edge. No, they had to come through the grounds.

He'd given orders to take at least one of them alive. He wanted to confront them, to make sure they knew they were responsible for the destruction that was about to happen. Things could still go wrong. It was still possible that war might not start. But at least he would have the satisfaction of knowing his brother's murderers had paid.

In the unlikely event his enemies somehow got past all the security, they would find him in this room. They'd be confident, seeing just an old, dying man, sitting in a chair. But he had a surprise in store for them, if it came to that.

Haltman's mind was a jumble of thoughts and images. He stood and winced with pain, then walked over to a desk and picked up a picture of Carissa.

Things could have been different, he thought. *If you'd lived. If that animal hadn't taken you.*

He held the picture up to his forehead for a moment, remembering, then set it back on the desk. The window coverings used to block the daytime sun were open. Outside, the wet stones of the patio glistened under the landscaping lights.

He decided he needed a drink. The doctors had warned him about mixing alcohol with the powerful cocktail of drugs he consumed every day. Well, the doctors had said a lot of things. Everything except what he wanted to hear, that a cure had been discovered or a new drug that would delay the inevitable.

Haltman went to a tall liquor cabinet in the corner of the room. He took out a bottle of cognac distilled from grapes grown on a sunlit hillside in France during the nineteenth century. It was the only bottle left in existence of that particular year and lineage. There didn't seem to be much point in letting it get any older. He broke open the wax seal and extracted the cork. He took a large, crystal snifter from the cabinet, filled it half full with the liquor, and returned to his chair.

He reached for another pill and swallowed it with some of the cognac. Somewhere at the edge of his jangled awareness, he heard the sound of a plane passing in the night.

CHAPTER 49

Nick, Lamont and Ronnie waited in the back of the plane. It had plenty of room. The Cessna was big enough to carry eight or nine passengers in addition to the pilot. This one had been modified for skydiving with the rollup door.

Nick activated his microphone.

"Selena, you copy?"

"You're five by five, Nick."

"Where are you?"

"I just passed Haltman's place. I'm about to turn around and head back."

"We're coming up on the drop zone any moment now."

"The fog is getting thicker," Selena said. "Be careful."

The voice of the pilot came over the comm link. "Two minutes."

"See you soon," Nick said. "Out."

Lamont pulled open the rollup door. Nick and Ronnie lined up behind him. The cabin filled with the noise of the engine and the air rushing by.

"Go in five," the pilot said over the comm link. "Four. Three. Two. One."

Lamont dove out of the open door, followed by Nick and Ronnie. The slipstream buffeted them, then was gone as the Cessna disappeared into the night.

They popped chutes and steered for the target.

Below, the white froth of the ocean broke in a ragged line against the rocky coast. The pilot had done a good job. Haltman's house was below them in the mists, outlined by landscaping lights. The patio where they would land was visible through the shifting fog.

A gust of wind tried to send Nick into the swimming pool. He steered clear and came down hard near the diving board. His ankle twisted under him as he struck the stones. Pain shot up his leg and into his lower back. He rolled, released the chute and stood, testing the ankle. It hurt, but he could walk on it. As long as he kept moving, it would be okay. He could feel the muscles in his back trying to lock up. It had given him trouble since a bad landing in Tibet.

They'd landed at one end of the house. They ran to a set of glass doors opening onto the patio. A single light shone inside the room. Nick guessed it was a guest bedroom. He slid the door open on quiet rollers and they stepped inside. No one was inside the room.

Lamont spoke in a quiet voice. "That was easy."

"Yeah," Nick said. "Maybe too easy. Remember what Freddie said."

In the room at the other end of the house, where Haltman was sipping from his crystal snifter, a red light began blinking on the wall over the monitors.

Haltman picked up a handheld radio and spoke into it. "They're here. The blue bedroom."

Two clicks sounded an acknowledgment.

Ronnie waited by the door of the bedroom, his hand on the knob. Nick nodded and Ronnie pulled the door open.

The bedroom was at the end of a hall leading away to the right, toward the rest of the house. Across the hall another door opened to a second bedroom. Lamont crouched down and covered the hall. Nick and Ronnie slipped across and into the bedroom.

"Clear," Nick said.

He came out of the room. The hall was spacious, with a high ceiling. It was ten feet wide, carpeted from wall-to-wall with thick pile and lined with expensive paintings in carved, gold frames. The only light came from lamps hung over the art.

Nick looked down the hall.

It's a shooting gallery. If I remember the plans right, this opens out into the main living area.

He signaled with his hand. They moved toward the living room. Ronnie heard a sound and glanced back, his MP-7 up at his shoulder. One of Haltman's guards stepped out of the bedroom they'd used to enter the house. Ronnie opened fire, a three round burst that caught the careless guard full in the chest. He fell back into the room.

Two men appeared at the other end of the hall. Nick and Lamont dropped down and opened up as the men fired.

The noise from the guards' guns drowned out the coughing stutter of the MP-7s. Two of the paintings blew from the wall. The frames shattered, sending a cloud of splinters through the air. Bullets gouged into the walls on either side. The two guards went down under the hail of bullets Nick and Lamont sent toward them.

"That's torn it," Nick said. "Move. Haltman's in here somewhere."

Selena heard everything over the comm link as she waited in the Suburban.

They ran into the main living area. Couches, chairs and end tables were scattered about the room. A light shone on a large oil painting hung over a mission style sideboard. A wall of windows twelve feet high faced out toward the back and the patio.

"Outside," Ronnie yelled.

Four more men were sprinting across the flagstones. Nick, Ronnie and Lamont turned as one toward the patio and fired. The windows exploded in a cascade of falling glass. The noise was intense, a strange symphony of breaking glass, the chatter of the guns, and shots and cries coming from the men outside. The couch next to Nick exploded in a cloud of stuffing as bullets ripped into it.

Lamont cried out and went down. A cold wind blew in through the shattered windows, bringing tendrils of fog and the salt odor of the ocean, mixed with the pungent smell of burnt powder.

One of the men on the patio was twisting on the ground in pain. Nick put two more rounds into him. He stopped moving.

Nick swiveled to cover Ronnie, bending over Lamont.

"I'm okay." Lamont took a painful breath and looked down at a hole in his shirt. "Sucker hit the armor."

"Take two aspirin and call me in the morning," Ronnie said.

He helped Lamont to his feet.

"We'll keep going," Nick said.

They passed a formal dining room with a long, polished table and entered another hallway leading toward the far end of the house.

The next room was the kitchen. Nick got down on one knee and glanced around the corner. A prepping island and grill took up the middle of the large room. Shining, copper bottomed pots and pans hung from a rack above it.

He ducked back as bullets splintered the frame of the door.

Ronnie reached down, drew out a grenade and lobbed it through the door. The explosion ripped the fancy cookware from the ceiling and sent shrapnel flying into the high-end appliances scattered about the room. Nick looked around the corner again. No more shots came from within.

They moved past two more empty rooms toward the end of the house, where it formed a right angled L at the end of the patio. Light came from around the corner. Music came from somewhere ahead. Someone was humming along with it.

Nick looked around the corner into a large room that took up the entire end of the house. A rack of computer monitors lined a wide shelf on the far wall, displaying images of the grounds. Someone was seated in a large, leather chair, his back turned toward the entrance. He had a glass in one hand. The other was moving in time to the music.

Then Nick realized he was looking at an image of himself looking around the corner on one of the monitors.

"I wouldn't advise coming any closer," Haltman said.

He swiveled his chair around.

"Why don't you all come out where I can see you?"

Nick and the others stepped out. Lamont watched the hall for more trouble.

"Let's see," Haltman said. "You're Carter, aren't you? And that brown looking man with the big nose must be the Indian."

Ronnie raised his weapon and stepped forward.

"You really shouldn't take another step, you know. Allow me to show you why."

Haltman set his drink down and picked up a piece of paper. He held it up to show them it was only paper, nothing more. He crumpled it into a ball.

"Watch carefully," he said.

He touched a button on the arm of his chair. Instantly, the opening filled with narrow, crisscrossing beams of red light.

He tossed the ball toward them. Just before it reached them, it burst into flame. The ashes dropped to the floor.

"Lasers," Haltman said. "My own design. Effective, don't you think?"

"Give it up, Haltman," Nick said. "There's nowhere for you to go."

"Nowhere for you, either."

"Nick," Lamont said. He gestured with his rifle.

Ten feet down the hall they'd just passed through, a second grid of red laser beams blocked their return. They were trapped.

"Do I have your attention?" Haltman asked.

"What do you want, Haltman? You know it ends here."

"Want?" Haltman's eyes were wild. "There's nothing I want from you except to watch you die. Like you watched my brother."

He giggled.

"Asshole is stoned," Lamont muttered under his breath.

"Your brother was a traitor and a murderer," Nick said. "He got what he deserved."

"Yes, you would say that, wouldn't you?"

Haltman picked up what might have been a television remote control, except it was larger and seemed to have more buttons than normal.

"I now call your attention to the central monitor on the top row," he said. He clicked on a button.

The picture on the monitor changed from a camera overlooking the front gate to an overhead satellite view of a broad expanse of snow covered ground. Tiny dots on the ground might have been buildings.

"You are looking at the Eastern Ukraine," Haltman said.

He clicked another button. A second monitor lit next to the first.

"Romania. What do you see, Carter? Oh, wait a minute, let me zoom in."

The images expanded as Haltman entered another command. As the lenses zoomed in, Nick recognized what he was looking at.

THAAD missile installations, the new deployments of America's latest system, set up as part of the highly touted European Shield.

"What do you think would happen if those missiles were fired into Russia?," Haltman said. "Please, humor me."

"You know damn well what would happen," Nick said. "It could start a war."

Haltman held up the remote.

"I designed the guidance system. I left a little something in the programming, just in case it might come in handy some day."

"What are you talking about?"

Haltman waved the remote back and forth.

"Do you see this button here? The big red one? I really couldn't resist making it red. If I push this button, all of those lovely missiles will take to the air. Can you imagine their surprise in Washington? In Moscow?"

"He's serious," Ronnie said.

"That's right, Tonto, I'm serious."

"You know I can't let you do that," Nick said.

"Right now you're probably thinking of shooting me and worrying about the lasers later. But that won't work, you see. I thought of that. Perhaps you've noticed that I haven't let go of this controller since I picked it up. If I let go, the missiles will launch. If I press the red button, the missiles will launch."

He smiled at them.

"My, my, whatever will you do?"

Outside the estate, Selena had heard every word as she sat in the car. Now she spoke into her microphone.

"Nick, don't show any sign. It sounds as though he's got you penned in with some kind of electronic trap, is that right? Cough once for yes, twice for no."

Nick coughed.

"I'm coming. Stall him."

Cough.

Her MP-7 was on the passenger seat next to her. She rolled down her window, started the engine, switched on the bright beams and pulled out onto the highway. She picked up speed, came to the entrance to the estate, and swung a hard right onto the drive.

Selena put her foot down on the accelerator. The outer chain-link fence appeared out of the mists. She kept her foot down, ducked, and drove the truck at speed into the double gates. They flew open with the sound of tearing metal, ripping off a fender and one of the headlights.

It was a quarter-mile from the outer gate to the stone wall. The drive was a dark, straight line cutting across the manicured grounds around it. She kept her foot down on the accelerator. The car shook, the steering wheel vibrating in her grip. A loud, screeching noise came from the engine compartment. Steam rose from the radiator. The battered vehicle would never be able to break through the heavy iron gate in the wall ahead. Haltman's guards would be at the guardhouse waiting for her. By now, they had to know she was coming.

Whoever designed the estate had made a mistake. The guardhouse was placed outside the wall instead of behind it, where it would have been protected. The lights in the guardhouse were on. Four men with submachine guns stood in front of the gate. They began shooting at her.

Selena ducked as bullets from the guns smashed through the windshield. She grabbed her weapon from the seat, opened her door and rolled out of the speeding truck. The ground was soft from rain, but still hard enough to knock the wind out of her. Knife-like pain wracked her injured thigh. She rolled, clutching the MP-7. The suburban hurtled toward the wall and smashed into the gate, scattering the men firing at her.

The gas tank ruptured and exploded, lighting the night with fire. Burning gas enveloped two of the guards. One rolled on the ground, trying to put out the flames. One man ran screaming into the darkness, a human torch.

Selena got to her knee. The last two guards were illuminated by the flames. She shot them before they recovered from the blast. She stood and limped as fast as she could toward the broken gate.

Inside the house, Nick, Ronnie and Lamont had heard everything over the comm link and watched on a monitor as the Suburban hurtled toward the gate. The camera had gone dark when the vehicle struck.

Haltman's right eye began twitching as he faced them.

"It won't make any difference," he said. "She won't get here in time. I assume it's your lovely wife, Carter? Even if she did, she couldn't get past the lasers. We wouldn't want to fry that little being inside her, would we?"

"What?" Lamont said.

"How did you know about that?" Nick said.

"I've been keeping an eye on you. I have many friends, Carter, in many places. Not so hard to obtain medical records, even if they're in Russian."

"Selena is pregnant?" Ronnie asked.

"Yeah."

"Well, Tonto? Aren't you going to offer congratulations?"

"You know, you really are an asshole," Ronnie said.

"Sticks and stones..." Haltman said.

"He's bluffing," Lamont said. "Shoot him."

"Let me demonstrate how this button works," Haltman said.

"Wait," Nick said. "I believe you. But I don't understand why you're doing it. I understand you think we're responsible for your brother's death. We're not, but I don't think I can convince you of that."

"Got that right," Haltman said. He giggled again.

"Okay. You want to punish us. But why start a war? It's kind of overkill, don't you think? Besides, the missiles on that system don't blow up. They're designed to destroy an incoming missile on impact, not land and set off a big explosion."

"Very good," Haltman said. "You're right, those missiles don't explode. But these do."

He pressed the button on his controller and a third monitor lit. It showed what appeared to be another THAAD installation.

"This is in Poland," Haltman said. "Take a good look, Carter."

Nick studied the image. Something wasn't right. Then he realized what it was.

"Those are cruise missiles. Tomahawks, nuclear tipped. There aren't supposed to be any offensive ground missiles in Europe."

"Go to the head of the class, Carter. It seems that someone in the Pentagon has been concealing things from your president. When I press this button, those will be launched along with the defensive missiles at the other locations. I expect the Russians will be quite upset when they see all those pretty streaks on their radar screens. They won't know which one to shoot down first. What would you do, if you were in their shoes?"

I'd retaliate, Nick thought. *Shit, he's got nukes pointed at them.*

Outside on the grounds, Selena limped as fast as she could toward the building. She didn't see the dog until it leapt at her with a low growl. She fired as the beast landed on her and knocked her down. The dog twitched and lay still.

It made her angry, that someone would take an animal and turn it into a killing machine. It helped fuel her will to get past the pain and keep going.

She was thinking about the plans to the house. If she remembered correctly, a panel controlling all the electrical power going into the building was located in the garage. If she cut the power, she'd take the lasers off-line. She spoke into her comm unit.

"Nick, I'm heading for the garage and the power. Keep him talking."

A single cough sounded in her ear piece.

The adrenaline surge was running out. A sudden wave of fatigue tried to overwhelm her. She pushed on, using the pain in her leg to keep going.

The garage was big enough for a second home. It featured three sets of arched, wooden doors and walls of stone. The parking apron in front of the garage was lit, but the interior was dark. She hoped there were no more guards or dogs to deal with. As she approached the garage, she changed out the magazine in her HK for a fresh one. She worked the charger and moved toward an entry door on the side of the building. She tried the handle.

Locked.

Screw this, she thought.

She stepped back and put a three round burst into the lock, then pushed the door open. A half dozen expensive cars were lined up inside, partly illuminated by light coming through windows in the garage doors. She moved toward the back of the garage, past a silver Bentley, looking for the power panel.

It has to be in here somewhere. Probably painted gray.

She saw what she was looking for next to a long workbench. Tools hung in orderly rows over the workbench.

"Don't move, bitch," a voice said behind her.

Most people would have done as they were told. Instead of freezing in place, Selena dropped and turned and fired at a man standing next to a low-slung Corvette. He fired as her rounds struck home. The bullets went over her head and into the rack of tools, sending wrenches and sockets flying. They made ringing, metallic noises as they bounced on the parked cars and the cement floor.

She waited to see if there were any others, then got painfully to her feet. She went over to the gray panel and opened it. Rows of circuit breakers greeted her, lined up one above the other.

Which one fed current to the lasers? She had no time to experiment. Selena moved back from the panel.

"Nick," she said, "get ready. I'm taking out the power."

She raised her MP-7 and fired. The result was spectacular. The panel erupted with cascades of orange sparks and arcing, violet-white light. The interior of the garage went dark as the lighting outside failed.

After images danced in her eyes. Sparks and crackling noises came from the panel. A tongue of flame crawled in a line up the side of the wall. In a minute, the wall was burning. Acrid smoke seeped out into the garage, smelling of burnt insulation. She coughed and limped back out into the air.

Inside the house, everything had gone dark.

"No!" Haltman shouted.

Then an emergency generator started up.

The lights flickered and came back on, along with the monitors. But the laser beams were gone. Nick and the others stepped into the room and stopped a few feet away from Haltman's chair.

"Stop," Haltman said. He had his finger over the red button.

"Don't do it," Nick said. "Please."

Haltman looked at him and Nick knew he'd lost.

"That's what Carissa must have said." He pressed the button.

On the monitors where the live satellite feed displayed the THAAD deployments, the systems came alive. Nick watched in horror as the platforms swiveled and elevated.

Flame and smoke shot from the back of the missiles as they streaked away toward Russia.

Haltman began laughing. His hand slipped down into his chair and came up with a pistol.

Ronnie shot him.

"Who the hell is Carissa?" Lamont asked.

CHAPTER 50

Nick looked down at Haltman's body and then back at the empty missile launchers on the monitors. Then he took out his satellite phone and called Harker.

"Yes, Nick." Her voice sounded clogged with sleep.

"Director, it's a code red. Haltman just launched missiles at Russia. Some of them are nukes."

"What?"

Any trace of sleep had disappeared from her voice.

"He triggered the THAAD deployments in the Ukraine and Romania. Plus one in Poland armed with Tomahawks."

"When?"

"About a minute ago."

"Where's Haltman?"

"Dead."

"All right." She disconnected.

In Virginia, Elizabeth thought hard and fast. The Pentagon would already know something had happened. They would inform the president. The missiles would trigger the Russian defenses. Orlov would retaliate, probably with his newly deployed medium-range cruise missiles. That in turn would require a larger response. It wouldn't be long until things went out of control.

What could she do? The world was minutes away from war. Her encrypted satellite phone was on the bedside table, where she always kept it at night. She picked up the phone. Her finger hovered over the button that would connect her to President Rice..

If the Russians knew why the missiles had been launched, if they knew it wasn't a deliberate act ordered by Washington, it might be stopped. But how to convince them it was the work of a madman and not the opening shots of world war?

Vysotsky. Call Vysotsky.

She entered Vysotsky's number and glanced at her clock. It was a little after four in the morning, which meant it was after five in the afternoon in Russia. Vysotsky would be awake, probably at his office in Yasenevo. After one ring, he picked up.

"Da."

"General, it's Elizabeth Harker."

"You have nerve calling, Director. Your country has launched an unprovoked attack upon us. You will regret it. I am too busy to talk to you now."

"Wait, General. That's why I'm calling. We didn't do it. This must be stopped before it gets out of control."

She could hear background noise that told her Vysotsky was in a car.

"We know they are your missiles," Vysotsky said. "Do you deny this?"

"I don't deny it," Harker said, "but we did not launch them. Someone else did."

Vysotsky laughed, an ugly, angry sound with no humor in it.

"Oh? A rogue commander, perhaps? Do you seriously expect me to believe this?"

"Hear me out," Elizabeth said. "I understand your anger, I would feel the same way. Let me explain."

"I am on my way to the Kremlin, Director. I will give you two minutes to convince me."

It wasn't much time to prevent the end of the world. Elizabeth took a breath and began. Five minutes later, Vysotsky was still listening.

"Haltman is dead," Elizabeth said. "There will be no more missile launches, unless you retaliate. If you do, it will be impossible to stop. Our two countries will be at war. You know what that means. Please, General, you must speak with Orlov and get him to hold off until this can be straightened out. Shoot them down but don't retaliate."

Elizabeth waited. Over her phone, she heard only Vysotsky's breathing and the sound of the car as it sped toward the ancient fortress of the Kremlin.

Finally, he said, "I will speak with our president."

Vysotsky disconnected.

Elizabeth's next call was to President Rice.

"Yes, Director. I don't have much time, I'm moving to Marine One and then Kneecap."

Marine One was the helicopter assigned to the president on a twenty-four hour basis. Kneecap was the designation for Air Force One in time of war. It was a complete, airborne command center, away from the nuclear bull's-eye that was Washington.

"Mister President, I have discovered who launched the missiles. There are nuclear tipped Tomahawks among them."

"Those missiles came from THAAD sites. They're defensive, unarmed. We don't have any cruise missiles stationed on the ground in Europe."

"Sir, that's not entirely true. A site in Poland was disguised as a THAAD installation but was armed with Tomahawks. The missiles were triggered by the man who designed software for the guidance systems."

Elizabeth took a breath. "Sir, on my own I contacted the Russians and explained what happened. We may still be able to avoid war if Orlov keeps his head about him."

She heard people yelling in the background.

"You talked with Orlov?" Rice asked.

Elizabeth heard the beat of rotors over the phone. Rice was approaching Marine One.

"No sir, I spoke with General Vysotsky. He was on his way to the Kremlin."

"Very well. I'll talk with you again when I'm in the air."

Rice disconnected.

Nothing to do now but wait and pray, Elizabeth thought.

CHAPTER 51

Nick sat next to Selena on the couch in their loft, looking out over the Potomac River. He had his arm around her shoulder. A Paul Kleé painting hung over the couch, a gift Selena had given him when he still lived in his apartment.

It was early evening. A bottle of wine sat on a coffee table in front of them.

"Rice is going to give us a medal," Nick said. "Of course we don't get to wear it, just hold it for a little bit until they put it away somewhere."

"We don't deserve a medal. We didn't stop that bastard from launching those missiles."

"No, we didn't. But we knew what had happened. That meant I could tell Harker and she could tell the Russians. If she hadn't gotten hold of Vysotsky, we wouldn't be sitting here. That river down there would be glowing in the dark."

"It was close, wasn't it?"

"I thought I was the one that understated things," Nick said.

Selena picked up her glass and drank.

"Is it all right for you to drink that now?"

"You mean the baby?"

"Yes. Junior."

"What if it's a girl?"

"You're not answering my question."

"After saving the world, I'm entitled to one glass of wine. But it's the last one for a while."

"We were really lucky," Nick said. "If one of those Tomahawks had gotten through, Moscow would've gone up in a mushroom cloud. As it was, some of the THAAD missiles did a lot of damage when they hit."

"I imagine the Pentagon is busy analyzing the Russian defense system," Selena said. "It's a lot better than we thought it was."

"That's not all they're analyzing. First they had General Sanford handing over plans to North Korea, then it turns out there's a rogue element in the Pentagon that thinks we should have nuclear tactical weapons on the ground in Europe. Their little stunt just blew the whole nuclear proliferation treaty to hell."

"Maybe in the end it'll be a good thing," Selena said. "Everyone will be forced to go back to the negotiating table after this. Who knows, we might even get an agreement to reduce these weapons."

"Yeah, maybe."

Nick refilled his glass.

"We need to talk. About you and the team."

"I know. When I was driving toward that gate, I wasn't thinking about much except going through it without getting killed. But afterward, I started thinking about us. I could've lost the baby. I don't know why I didn't. I hit the ground pretty hard when I jumped out of that truck."

"You can't go into the field anymore."

"We talked about this before. Even if I hadn't gotten pregnant, it was time. I want to go back to the languages, studying and translating ancient writings. Teaching people about them. I'm good at it and I miss it. It's less exciting than chasing down assholes like Haltman, but in its own way it's just as challenging."

"We'll still work together," Nick said. "The only difference is you're back in a consulting role. Like when we met."

"I hope not quite like when we met. That wasn't the most peaceful day I've ever had. I really loved that car."

Selena snuggled up against him.

"What are we going to name him?" Nick asked.

"Her," Selena said. "What are we going to name her?"

NOTES

The world the project works in may be
fictional, but it is based on real-life possibilities and
events. I weave things that are real with things that
are not in these stories. For example, *Black Dolphin*
may or may not be real, but underwater drones do
exist. It doesn't take much imagination to see how
they could be used for destructive purposes.

High Alert is an actual military designation and
refers to a state of instant readiness for war. All of
our missiles are on permanent High Alert.

They are working hard in Pyongyang to build
an offensive nuclear option and are making
progress. There is no doubt the regime possesses
nuclear weapons. Not many, but how many do you
need? It is also a distinct possibility that they are
about to or have already tested a small,
thermonuclear device. Such a device would be
difficult to detect. One can only hope they have not
developed the technology to create a version of the
factual Russian 'Tsar Bomba.' If a bomb like that
was detonated above the United States, it would set
the clock back to 1850.

The new, two stage missile engine described in
the book exists. It remains to be seen how long it
will take North Korea to install it on an ICBM.
Some experts believe Pyongyang already has
missiles capable of reaching North America and
Europe. It seems clear that the North now has
missiles capable of reaching Japan.

As far as I know, the special Russian stealth
helicopter described in the book does not exist.
However, the MI-35M helicopter is real, a lethal

evolution of the famous Hind that caused so much trouble in Afghanistan.

There has been much talk of Moscow moving their SS-20 (called the Iskander) intermediate-range missiles to the Ukrainian border in response to U.S. THAAD deployments in Eastern Europe. They may have been installed in Kaliningrad. This would be a direct violation of the nuclear proliferation treaty. To the best of my knowledge, the United States no longer keeps tactical nuclear weapons in Europe. The Pentagon doesn't really need the land-based weapons. There are plenty of nuclear cruise missiles mounted on the mobile platform provided by our naval forces.

The satellite launch site at Musudan-Ri is real. I made a few changes, but tried to describe it as accurately as possible without visiting it in person, something of course impossible to do. I have been to South Korea, so perhaps that lends a kind of distant authenticity.

The South Blade unit mentioned in the story is real. China's special forces are good and getting better. The People's Republic has been upgrading their military for years. The wisdom of having a highly professional force trained in the military arts needed to confront today's unconventional threats is beyond question. Our units are the best in the world, but there are others, like the Russian *Spetsnaz*, that can give them a run for the money. Special Forces are the pinnacle for a professional warrior. At that level of training and competence, the flag on one's shoulder makes little difference.

I hope you have enjoyed this book.
Alex Lukeman
March, 2017

ACKNOWLEDGEMENTS

Always first, my wife, Gayle. No one who doesn't live with a writer can understand how difficult it can be. Her support is much better than gold.

Bill Hammerton, Paula Howard and Gloria Lakritz for their help in spotting problems before publication.

All the people I've never met who fill the internet with informative articles, research and (sometimes) useful opinions.

You, the reader. There's not much point in being a writer if you aren't there turning pages. Thank you.

ABOUT THE AUTHOR

Alex Lukeman writes thrillers featuring a covert intelligence unit called the PROJECT. Alex is a former Marine and psychotherapist and uses his experience of the military and human nature to inform his work. He likes riding old, fast motorcycles and playing guitar, usually not at the same time. You can email him at alex@alexlukeman.com. He loves hearing from readers and promises he will get back to you.

http://www.alexlukeman.com

The PROJECT Series

White Jade
The Lance
The Seventh Pillar
Black Harvest
The Tesla Secret
The Nostradamus File
The Ajax Protocol
The Eye of Shiva
Black Rose
The Solomon Scroll
The Russian Deception
The Atlantis Stone
The Cup
High Alert

Be the first to know when I have a new book coming out by subscribing to my newsletter. No spam or busy emails, only a brief announcement now and then. Just click on the link below. You can unsubscribe at any time...

http://bit.ly/2kTBn85

CPSIA information can be obtained
at www.ICGtesting.com
Printed in the USA
BVHW03s0825280518
517491BV00019B/1132/P